J.P. Grider

Maybe This Life

Published by Fated Hearts Publishing

1st Edition Copyright 2012 J.P. Grider
2nd Edition Copyright 2013 J.P. Grider
Cover Design by Brian Scully

ISBN: 978-1477498125

Dedicated to my Nana, the real Angelina Maria, and to my beautiful grandmother, Bette and my dearly missed grandfather, Sam.

J.P. Grider

Chapter One

Lena jolted awake rattled and dripping with sweat. Reaching for her pillow and feeling it beneath her palm, she tried to calm down. The room was pitch-black and empty. Aside from her pounding heart trying to claw its way out of her chest, she remained still. "Breathe, Lena. Breathe," she told herself. It was only a dream, that's all. A dream. Another dream. Another nightmare invading her sleep like a bad horror flick.

When would they stop? Every night, Lena's sleep was interrupted by these familiar strangers. These unwelcome intruders who terrorized her nights with constant images of assault on the same poor female victim. And the teenage boy who just stands there, drained of life, drained of emotion, looking on but doing nothing. It was always the same. The girl, running from apparent attackers. The boy, watching in fear, yet paralyzed with terror and unable to come to her rescue.

This night, Lena tried to calm herself but found it impossible. Keeping focused on her breathing, Lena attempted to close her eyes. Once she felt her heart rate return to normal, she was still unable to get back to sleep, afraid she'd begin the nightmares all over again.

But she needed sleep. Tomorrow morning was her interview with the NNJCC and God knew... she needed this job. It had been three years since her graduation from Seton Hall University, and she still held her position as a drive-thru bank teller. Not that there was anything wrong with being a teller, but it wasn't Lena and it certainly wasn't what her parents intended when they paid a substantial sum of money for Lena to get a degree in Television and Film Production. Of course the perfect job had come along months ago, but Vince made her turn it down. A job as Production Assistant in New York City was God-sent, but it would have been selfish of Lena to accept a job that would take her away from Vince for too long. So here was Lena, preparing for an interview as a Public Relations Coordinator at Northern New Jersey Cable Company. Not exactly the exciting land of make-believe that the television world provided, but it was a nine-to-five position. And most importantly, it pacified Vince.

After hours of gazing at the ceiling fan going around and around, the repetition of the blades finally rendered her bored enough to drift into a dreamless slumber. A slumber, free from the horror of her previous nightmare. The buzzing of the alarm clock came much too soon. It jostled Lena from her sleep and left her staring into a brightly lit, sun-drenched room.

Her interview was in two hours, and she needed to pry her tired eyes open. After ambling into the kitchen to get a cup of coffee from her Keurig, she took a couple sips and dragged herself into the shower with only the cold water running. The ice-cold stream of water held her only hope of manipulating her tired muscles after a restless night's sleep. Once the cold water shocked her system awake, Lena turned the knob to the left to allow hot water to cascade over her and melt her consternations away.

Absentmindedly massaging the shampoo into her scalp, Lena's thoughts splashed back to last night's harrowing dream. Her sleep-induced vision of a teenage girl tied to her bedpost and beaten with a leather strap was frighteningly too real for Lena. She tried to shake the image from her mind but realized that there was something too familiar about the people in her dream. Could the nightmare be a manifestation of unexpected events in Lena's life? Or could the girl in her dreams be real? It was always the same girl – the same, familiar, cherubic face. But what about the boy? In every dream or nightmare, the same boy stood watching. Eyes wide and mouth pinched, coming in and out of focus, he always ignored her plea for help.

The hot water had now run cold, bolting Lena out of her stupor. There was no more time to analyze her nightmare; she needed to get to her interview. She dried herself off, got herself a new cup of hot, steaming coffee, and sipped it while she looked over her resume. Once she let the coffee settle in her empty stomach, Lena went to her room to dress. Her favorite navy-blue knee-length sailor dress, navy tights, and matching flats felt comfortable, but she still took one last look in the mirror. The three-quarter length sleeves of her dress came just above the wrist, long enough to cover the bruises on her forearms. She smiled. Good. No one would see them. Then she decided to slide a thin, navy headband into her long, straight black hair to polish off the professional look. She placed her hand over the half of a heart-shaped locket that hung from the gold chain around her neck, brought it to her lips, kissed it for good-luck, and dashed out the door into her electric-green Ford Focus.

When she inserted the key into the ignition, she froze. Is this what she wanted? If they offered her the job, would she take it? It wasn't a high-profile position or a foot-in-the-door to a television project, but it was in the P.R. department of the local cable company, and cable *was* an aspect of television.

There was that nagging notion in the back of her head though. Was this job what *she* wanted? Or was it what *Vince* wanted? Lena always believed that things happened for a reason, but what if she ended up going against fate? She hadn't taken the position she really wanted; could she trust that it just wasn't meant to be? Whatever was ahead for her, would it be her destiny to be there or would she be living a lie?

Chapter Two

Rick Murphy sat in absolute darkness, like he did every night, attempting to summon up his past and reach the woman he left behind -the woman he hadn't the chance to save from the violent world in which she belonged. His efforts to conjure up her image were mostly fruitless. Bits and pieces of memories from an expired life was all he had of her. His heart felt as stark as the room he occupied.

It had been years since he'd allowed anyone access to his heart, vowing to love only the woman who bore possession of his soul. He attempted to embrace other women, but none of those relationships had lasted. Not one woman had lived up to the woman he'd left behind. Rick never intended to discard the affections of one of his lovers. On the contrary. In the beginning of a courtship, Rick aspired to giving one hundred percent of himself to the new relationship. But although he was there in mind and body, his heart and soul were adrift somewhere in the past.

His memory never failed at recalling the pivotal moment when Angie reentered his life. He was twelve years old. He remembered it like it was yesterday, not twenty-five years ago. It had been warm for early October. Rick recalled this ordinarily inconsequential fact, because on October 10, 1986 at exactly 9:36a.m. on his Swatch watch, Rick sensed an almost transcendent experience when, as he took a drag off his first cigarette, he felt an icy chill run up his spine. At this same exact moment, a girl appeared sitting on a step that wasn't there. He was standing in the woods with three of his friends; all of them experimenting with their first cigarette and first time playing hooky from school.

"Did you guys just feel that?" Rick asked his three coughing delinquent friends.

"Feel what?" One of them choked out.

"That cold wind that just blew through."

But none of them had felt it. And none of them saw the girl...or the step.

After that fall day of firsts, Rick would see the girl frequently but in his mind only. The girl didn't exist, yet suddenly she had a name. Angie. And Angie had become part of his life from that point forward. At first, frightened by these images, Rick worried that something was very wrong with him. But over the years he had become comforted by her presence, realizing that Angie *did* exist in his life. Just not in *this* life.

In the dim room, Rick lit his fifth cigarette in the past hour, hoping to trigger a vision of Angie. The familiar scent of burning nicotine and the smoky-sweet taste of the filterless rolled tobacco were the frequent catalysts to revisiting his precious illusions. Rick had once made an effort to quit his unhealthy habit, but when he'd realized that Angie had dematerialized along with the absence of his Camel's, he picked up his former catalytic vice without delay. Tonight, however, he had not succeeded in reaching her. Instead, he decided to raise the window shades and get himself ready for work. He'd go about his day as he usually did, joylessly managing his headend and team of field technicians at NNJCC and hopelessly hungering for a love he could never have.

Chapter Three

Lena thundered through the parking lot threateningly close to being late for her interview. Spending too much time negotiating her future, her heart rate pumped at maximum pace. Though she now ran late, she allowed herself exactly three deep breaths before timorously stepping out of her car. Lena shuttered. Pulling into the space behind her, a black Jeep Wrangler, with its roof and doors missing, blared Van Halen from its speakers. Though it was unseasonably warm, Lena questioned why someone would have the roof off so early in the Spring. She assumed that was more of a Summer thing. But she soon stopped thinking anything when she saw the man who drove the Wrangler. Ambling out of the Jeep and through the lot was the most gorgeous dark-haired man she had ever seen. As he meandered toward her, Lena noticed the auburn sheen that glazed his thick, wavy brown hair and she couldn't help but be mesmerized by his bright green eyes, reminiscent of brilliant emerald stones. Already jumpy due to interview jitters, Lena was now on the verge of excitability. "Calm, Lena. Remain calm." Lena was in the habit of talking to herself when she was frightened or nervous. *Just shut the car door, and walk confidently into the building.* Lena kept up her pep-talk, but when she so calmly closed her car door, she *slammed* it shut…on her hand.

"Ouch," said an unfamiliar baritone voice. "That could *not* have felt good."

Lena turned to see him. The guy in the Wrangler. *Oh how humiliating.* Here was this gorgeous man, with dreamy eyes, staring at her...and laughing. Laughing *at* her? Probably. But oh those dimples. And that body – tall, lean, muscular, heavenly. His polo shirt fit just snug enough to hug those sinewy pecs. Oh my goodness, what was she thinking?

Her face flushed when she realized he had been still standing there in front of her waiting to hear if she was all right. She timidly filled him in. "Oh I'm okay, it's fine."

She noticed his reaction when his eyes met hers. He narrowed them as if trying to recall something and hesitated before speaking again. Wrangler let out an almost imperceptible sigh when he smiled back at her. "Let me take you inside. I'll get you an ice pack from the kitchen."

"No, really," Lena replied, "I'm fine. Uh, I'll be fine." She shook her head. "I…uh…," she didn't even know what she wanted to say. This man made her fluster, and she couldn't understand why.

"Okay. I hope your hand doesn't hurt too much," he gave a resigning smile as he held his gaze on her – an intense, electrifying gaze.

Lena was the first to break the awkward staring contest. "Uh, really, I, uh...need to get going." She felt his eyes follow her as she paced into the building.

While she sat in the waiting area for Dan Shoup, the PR Director, to come and escort her to his office, she couldn't help but think of the man she saw in the parking lot. Wrangler. Her face felt warm, and she was embarrassed by her own thoughts. She shouldn't be thinking about another man. She was engaged to marry Vince next October. Lena's father had already spent so much money on the down payment for The Brownstone House. She'd always dreamed of having her wedding reception in the old Brownstone House in Paterson, and her father made sure she would realize that dream. Not to mention the two thousand dollars he spent on her vintage gown. Lena tried to switch her thoughts from the dreamy man she just met outside. Since she didn't want to get herself more nervous by going over her interview questions for the hundredth or so time, she thought about when she'd first started going out with Vince. She tried to conjure up good thoughts, like when he first came to her house to meet her parents, and he came bearing the ingredients to make ice cream sundaes. He had told her afterwards that he knew it would be a good icebreaker. She remembered how happy she felt at that moment. How thoughtful he had been. Vince was a Battaglia. His family owned numerous shopping centers, and their financial weight in the Borough of Haledon was substantial. Lena wasn't too impressed with money, having grown up in an equally prominent family. Her family owned several liquor stores, one of them, the most popular in Haledon. But she'd taken notice of Vince when she had seen him around town, and he seemed like a nice guy. So when he'd asked her out on a date, she'd said yes immediately. However, her thoughts turned as ice cold as the ice-cream Vince had brought that day when she couldn't help but recall the emotional pain of the first time she had sex with him. Lena had never intended to 'go all the way.' She knew her parents expected her to wait until she was married before being intimate with a man, and that is what Lena had intended to do. Vince was more experienced when it came to physical intimacies, so she understood that waiting would be hard for him. But Vince never believed Lena when she had told him she was still a virgin. He said he couldn't comprehend how in this day and age someone would actually wait until his or her wedding night to have sex.

So on this particular night, Vince thought he would go further than their usual 'second base.'

They were stretched out on his bed, side by side. He gently slid his hand under her skirt and touched the inside of her thigh. Although it felt kind of nice, Lena took his hand away from beneath her skirt. She knew where it would lead, and she wasn't ready yet. Vince pulled away, looked into Lena's eyes, and gave her one of his seductive smiles. He moved closer so that he was on top of her and kissed her aggressively. Once again, Vince lifted up her skirt, slid his hand underneath, and pulled aside her panties. She put her hand on his arm to pull his hand away, but in the next instant, he turned rough, pushing open her thighs and forcing himself inside of her. Lena pushed Vince off of her and sat stunned in front of him.

"How...could you...do that...to me?...You knew I wanted to wait," Lena choked back her tears.

Vince had a smirk on his face when he saw the blood on his sheets. "Wow, I guess you weren't lying," was his only response.

Lena walked out that night wondering how she could trust Vince again. How could she date someone, let alone marry someone, who could think so little of what he did? He had violated her most private wishes. An elephant felt like it had landed on her chest, thinking about what she would face in the morning. Would her parents be able to tell? And how would she be able to look in the mirror and stare at a girl who had lost her innocence? She would never ever get it back again.

That night, Lena vowed she would end her engagement to Vince. At that moment, she had hated him for taking away her virginity before she was ready. She no longer wanted anything to do with him, but could she find the confidence to walk away?

The next day, however, Vince came to her apartment to apologize, and as was always the case, Lena forgave him, even though it was never really an apology. She remembered it as if it were yesterday.

"Lena, baby," he took her in his arms and looked her in the eyes. "I know I should have asked you first if you wanted to have sex, but I really thought you did. I am sorry, baby. Really. I misunderstand you sometimes, that's all. Next time, be more assertive with me so I know."

Lena tried to think of what to say, but no words came to her mind.

Vince continued on, "Listen, Lena, I said I was sorry. Really."

She placed her hands on his chest and pushed him away. "You're always sorry, Vinnie, but...," Lena trailed off, not knowing where to go with this.

Vince threw his hands up in the air then punched her wall, leaving a gaping hole the size of an orange in the sheet rock.

"Vince."

"Oh shut it, Lena," he was yelling now. "I'm not the only one in the wrong here. *You* walked out on *me* last night. We make love for the first time, and then you take off." His voice lowered to almost a whisper. "How do you think that made *me* feel? I was so happy to finally show you how much I love you. I have feelings too, Lena. You're my goddamn fiancé; I should be able to make love to you." Vince languidly sat on the couch and put his head in his hands. Lena saw his shoulders twitch and thought maybe he was crying.

Lena watched him for a moment. Make love for the first time? Is that what he called it? Was that really how making love felt? Forced and full of pain? But Lena saw him quivering like a baby and thought, *maybe he did misinterpret her intentions*. Maybe she wasn't clear enough when she told him she had wanted to wait until their wedding date. She shrugged to herself and walked over to Vince on the couch. "I'm sorry, Vince, I shouldn't have walked out."

Vince lifted his head and looked at Lena with his usual smugness. His eyes were completely dry. "Thanks, babe. Let's put this behind us, okay?" Vince held his arms out for Lena. She sat on the couch next to him and let him hold her, but she wasn't able to fall effortlessly into his arms. He had forced a wedge between them so deep that Lena imagined it would be impossible for her to ever feel the same towards him. Outwardly, their relationship went back to the way things were, but Lena's heart had turned hollow. A part of her had died that night. Vince had raped her of her innocence, but feeling lower than ever, Lena allowed Vince to take her over and over again from then on. She had lost the will to fight him on it and, in the end, lost her self-esteem as well. Over time, Lena had begun to feel as if she were just going through the motions of someone else's life.

Prompting her from her trance was the receptionist. "Mr. Shoup is ready to see you now. Please come with me, Ms. Giordano." Lena picked up her briefcase and purse to follow the woman to the elevator. "Mr. Shoup's office is the first office to the left of the elevator on the second floor."

Lena had thanked the woman and continued on to her interview.

Dan Shoup had hired Lena on the spot. He knew immediately that she would be perfect for the position of Public Relations' Coordinator. Dan had admitted that Lena's Seton Hall University education and her character and disposition were perfect for what he was looking for. Lena would be able to use her writing skills to prepare newsletters and press announcements, and she would use her bubbly personality at the many functions she would be coordinating for the town officials and local cable channels. Dan welcomed Lena to his PR team and hoped she'd be as happy at NNJCC as he was to have her there.

****

Rick sat in his office staring blankly into the television screen that hung from the wall in front of him. He had so much paperwork he needed to finish, but he could not stop thinking about the girl he met in the parking lot. At first he just thought she was another pretty, petite brunette, but when she'd turned in his direction, her beauty awed him. Her flawless, olive skin and her perky nose that drew attention to her heart-shaped lips were breathtaking. The little sailor dress she had on fit her tiny frame perfectly. And she had a refreshingly wholesome manner about her.

Rick had no idea why she was here. He knew she didn't work at the cable company; he would have certainly remembered seeing her walking around the building. She could have been a customer, but he had hoped not, considering he probably would never encounter her again if that were the case. Maybe a job interview? That would be awesome. He'd have to ask around to see if any positions were open. Damn. He should have gotten her name, then he could somehow find her. He needed to find her.

Chapter Four

"So, Babe, you excited about starting your new job tomorrow?" Vince asked Lena, who cuddled in his arms while they sat on her red plaid couch and watched the college basketball game on TV.

Lena shrugged. "I'm more nervous than excited."

"Aw, you don't need to be nervous. You'll just use those Seton Hall words of yours that I hate, and you'll impress those snobs at the cable company."

Lena didn't know if Vince complimented her or put her down. That's usually the way it was; he would dole out compliments freely, then he'd always add a slight twist to make her wonder what he really meant. She shrugged again. "I'll be fine, I guess." Lena wasn't as excited as she thought she'd be. She was happy to give up her bank teller job, but this PR position wasn't exactly the

Production Assistant position she could have had if Vince wasn't so controlling. Not standing up to him about that was turning out to be one of Lena's big regrets. She was afraid that her resentment towards Vince was growing too rapidly. Every time she saw a newly produced music video, she thought of her dream to produce an amazing rock video. Many producers started as production assistants and worked their way up through the crew. But now Lena thought that dream would never come true. Instead, she accepted a job writing press releases. Where was the fun in that? And where would it take her? Certainly not to some television studio.

There was *one* aspect of working at the local cable company that she looked forward to. The Wrangler guy. She couldn't get her mind off of him. Not that she tried too hard. She was sure he worked there, considering the way he'd offered to get her ice for her hand. She sure hoped he worked there. Lena couldn't wait to see him again. Those eyes. There was something about his green eyes that sent a chill through her. As much as her hand had been hurting when she'd slammed it in the car door, the adrenaline pumped so rapidly through her veins when she caught sight of Wrangler's eyes that she'd forgotten for a moment that she was in pain.

Never in her life had one look at someone caused such an immense reaction...and such a strong one. She felt so guilty about that. She shouldn't be attracted to anyone besides Vince. But she just couldn't help herself.

"Yeah! Yes! Did you see that play, Babe? Wooh-hooh, they did it. Did you see that?" Vince nudged Lena in the ribs, prompting her out of daydreaming about Wrangler. "They won, Babe. They did it. Shit yeah." He exclaimed

"Great." Lena really didn't care about basketball, but Vince did, so she followed it along with him. "Vince, do you mind if I get ready for bed? I'd like to get a good night sleep tonight."

"But it's not even eight o'clock. You're asking me to leave?"

Lena flinched before answering. "I'm sorry, Vince, I'm just really tired."

"Geez, Lena. You're not ten, it's not past your effin' bedtime."

"I know, Vince, I'm tired, that's all."

Vince's eyes bore into hers. "You're friggin' unbelievable, you know that?" Vince threw the remote across the room. "Go get your precious sleep, Lena." Vince stormed towards the door, and Lena heard him mumble, "Bitch," under his breath.

Lena shut the door behind him, picked up the drinks from her coffee table, and brought them to her kitchen sink. Then she got on her pajamas, brushed her teeth, and went to bed. She really did want a good night's sleep before starting her new job.

As Lena drifted off, her thoughts wandered back to the man from the parking lot. She couldn't get those emerald-green eyes out of her mind.

She saw him smile at her and then at a closer look, he was crying. A tear crawled down his cheek and he whispered good-bye. Had she been dreaming? She felt her body falling into a slumber. Suddenly she was sitting on the front steps of a row-style house while she waved good-bye to a man dressed in fatigues. He blew a kiss to her as his lips formed the words, 'Wait for me.'

It wasn't until Lena was showering the next morning that she recalled her dream. *That was odd,* she thought, but she soon chuckled as she realized how peculiar her imagination was. She didn't know if it was the coffee she usually drank late in the evening, or if her constant daydreaming conjured erratic night dreams. At least last night's visions were not like the senseless nightmares she'd been having recently. Lena was thankful for that.

The impressive drive through Franklin Lakes to get to NNJCC was lost on Lena, who could barely remember getting to work. Her sole focus had been on starting her new job this morning, which would begin in exactly ten minutes. She'd considered getting to work earlier, but decided against it when she thought maybe it'd appear as if she were too overzealous. Instead, she opted for reporting in only ten minutes early. As luck would have it, she'd arrived at precisely the time that Wrangler had pulled into the lot. That fact, along with the realization that he was practically jogging to catch up to her at the main entrance, added to Lena's jumble of nerves.

"Lena, wait up."

Shocked, she turned to him. "Uh, how did you know my name?"

He reached across her to open the door and allow her to enter before he followed after her. "I've asked about you." His smile was captivating. She actually felt her heart skip a beat.

"When?"

"That day I saw you in the parking lot."

"Oh." Was it flattering or just plain creepy? She opted to go with flattering. Knowing he was interested in her enough to wonder who she was caused a warm sensation to flow from her head down to her toes. What was wrong with her? What *were* these feelings?

The elevator door opened almost simultaneously to his pushing the button. They were the only two taking the ride up, making for a very uncomfortable trip as far as Lena was concerned. She was nervous enough starting her new job and all; being so close to a man who caused her heart to race was more than she could handle right now.

"I think you'll like it here, Lena. Your co-workers in the PR department are really cool, especially Gary and Lindsey."

The elevator door opened to the second floor. Wrangler seemed hesitant to leave. "By the way, I'm Rick. It's nice to have formally met you, Lena."

Rick. Lena never even thought to ask what *his* name was. Darn. Bad first impression. Correction. Second impression. First one was even worse.

"Lena." Dan Shoup, Lena's new boss, greeted her when she walked into the department.

"Hello, Mr. Shoup." *Darn. Too formal?*

"Oh please, call me Dan. We all go by first names here." Lena followed Dan into a small cubicle with a window situated behind a desk. "This is your desk. You can get situated, and I'll see you in my office in about fifteen minutes to go over your agenda."

"Okay, great." Lena put her purse in her new desk drawer and hung her coat on the hook on the wall, before exploring her new work area.

"Hey there. Lena, right?" A brown-haired man about Lena's age approached her desk and held out his hand.

Lena stood and shook his hand. "Yes."

"I'm Gary. I'm the other coordinator here." Gary turned when he heard footsteps. "Oh, and this is Lindsey. She's Dan's assistant."

"Hi, Lindsey. I'm Lena."

Lindsey looked to be in her thirties, but the severe bun in her blonde hair could have been misleading.

"Hey, you. I'm so glad we have another girl in the office. I hated being outnumbered." Yeah. Lena was sure it was the bun. When Lindsey spoke, she sounded much younger than thirty. "Hey, Lena, you should come out with us on Friday nights. Gary and I usually go with Betty from Engineering to watch Rick from Engineering play at The Tavern in town."

"Play?" Lena's ears perked up at the mention of Rick's name, if it was even the same Rick.

"Oh sure. Rick Murphy, the Engineering Manager plays guitar and keyboard, and every other instrument under the sun, while he sings. He has a gig every Friday night." Lindsey spoke so quickly, it was hard to catch what she said. *Definitely younger than thirty*, Lena thought. Was she dating Rick? Was Rick attracted to blond-haired girls? Lena hoped not, since her own hair was as dark as night. Wait a minute. Lena mentally shook her thoughts free. It may not have even been the same Rick and besides, Lena was marrying Vince at the end of the year. "So," Lindsey continued. "Ya think you might wanna join us?"

"It sounds like fun. Let me just check with my fiancé."

"Oh, you're engaged? That's wonderful. When?"

"October," Lena mumbled.

"You don't sound too excited. If it were me, I'd be going crazy with excitement." Lindsey was waving her arms exuberantly as she spoke.

"Lindsey," Gary interrupted. "You talk too much."

Gary took the words right out of Lena's mouth, but Lena liked Lindsey. She looked forward to working with such an energetic person. She'd make the workday fun, Lena thought. But she couldn't help but hope there was nothing between Lindsey and the same Rick that Lena was infatuated with. Suddenly, Lena's desire for Rick, and the guilt it involved, manifested as a painful knot in the pit of her stomach.

On the way home from work that evening, Lena felt that unusual pang in her heart – that sensation that swung somewhere between excitement and fear. She was excited about her new job and new co-workers but feared that her attraction to Rick would escalate and Vince would find out. Vince learning of her attraction to anyone or anything besides him would not be good.

When Lena got home to her apartment, her younger sister by three years pulled into the parking lot. "Hey Leen, I saw you pulling in, so I figured I'd stop and see how your first day went."

"Hey, Katrina." Leaning into the driver's side window, Lena's blond-haired, blue-eyed sister greeted her. "It was good. I think I'm going to like it."

"Yeah? That's cool. Hey, Joe wants to know if we're still getting together to go down the shore next weekend?"

"Oh, yeah. Not *this* Saturday, right?"

"No Lena, next. Why, what's this Saturday?"

"Oh, nothing...no, nothing at all. Friday night, um, I may be going out," Lena stammered.

"Whaddya mean? Without Vince?" Katrina seemed suspicious.

"Oh, I, um..I don't...I don't know, I..didn't tell him yet. So, where you off to?" Lena was quick to change the subject; her sister would definitely be able to see through to her feelings.

"Don't change the subject. Where you going Friday?" Katrina insisted.

After inhaling a long time, Lena finally answered, "No, just...with some co-workers, that's all."

Katrina said nothing, and this was usually a successful attempt at getting Lena to talk some more.

"We're just going to see...a guy...another co-worker. He's playing at The Tavern in Oakland."

"Aaah...and what's his name? This other co-worker."

Damn, Kat was good. "Uh, just...Rick...I think, um Rick Murphy, yeah." Lena felt her skin turn warm, and she was sure Katrina could see her blushing.

"Oh, well you go and enjoy Rick Murphy Friday night." She laughed.

"Katrina."

"No really, enjoy a night out with your friends. I'm serious...I just hope Vince *lets* you."

"Yeah...me too. See ya later, Kat."

"Yeah, love ya Leen."

Inching her way into her apartment, Lena was sure there'd be some type of problem with Vince letting her go out alone Friday night. There would always be some kind of problem where Vince was concerned.

Chapter Five

    Rick was more keyed up than usual before one of his Friday night gigs. Gary mentioned to him that Lena would be joining them for happy hour, and then she'd stay to watch Rick's performance. Usually cool and calm before a show, Lena's presence made him nervous. He wondered if she would enjoy his singing, or if she'd find it lame. After all, he was just a bar performer playing to a crowd for his own enjoyment. It's not like he was getting paid a whole heck of a lot, but he loved the feeling it gave him to sing and play his guitar. Or any instrument for that matter. Music fed his soul, and it relaxed him to play. Tonight, however, he found no relaxation in knowing Lena would be watching. But he was excited to see her.

    He went from excited and jittery to tense and agitated in the time it took the waitress to take the order and bring it to the table. This was how long it took Lena's fiancé to piss him off. First of all, Rick never thought to look at her left hand; *she's engaged,* he thought. Damn. He really wished she were available. Second, of course Rick expected Lena to come alone, and third, her fiancé Vinnie, or something like that, was an asshole. In the ten minutes Vinnie was there, Rick already wanted to punch the obnoxious ass. Curt, impolite and downright disparaging to Lena, Vinnie showed her no respect. Rick could not understand how a sweet, refined person like Lena could *be* with a person like that, never mind marry one.

"What's your problem, man?" Vinnie tossed his chin in Rick's direction, addressing the question at him. "You have a problem with me? I see the way you're looking at me."

Rick wanted to remain composed, but his blood boiled from listening to Vinnie's constant belittling of Lena. He tried to hold his tongue for Lena's sake when Vinnie called her a clumsy shit because she accidentally knocked over a glass of water when he elbowed her in the rib – all because she didn't introduce him to everyone quickly enough. Rick tried to steady his breathing and stay out of it when Vinnie decided to tell everyone that 'screwing Lena was like screwing a piece of wood.' But Rick could no longer disguise his disgust. He took one look at Lena's timid demeanor. She was biting her bottom lip and fumbling with the necklace she had around her neck. Vinnie embarrassed her. Rick wanted to remain calm to keep her from further humiliation, but the hatred he suddenly had for this man blinded him from Lena's immediate humility.

"As a matter of fact, *Vinnie*," Rick sneered. "I do have a problem with you. How you treat the woman you love is repulsive. It's sickening and insufferable. You are a vile man, and if it weren't for sparing Lena further embarrassment, I'd take you out right here."

"Rick." Gary nudged him.

Vinnie stood from the table. "You fuckin' shit." Vinnie raced around the table and threw a punch at Rick. Rick stopped him mid-punch by grabbing Vinnie's wrist before it hit his face.

"Vince, please," Rick heard Lena plead. Vinnie tried to throw a punch with his other fist, but Rick stopped that as well. By now all the other patrons had heard the wrangling, and the owner headed over.

"Rick, what's the problem here?"

"Nothing, Jack, it's under control." Rick answered The Tavern's owner without tearing his glare away from Vinnie.

"Let's get outta here, Lena. Your friend's an ass."

Lena looked at Rick and shrugged, and that's when he saw the pain and sadness in her eyes. Lena turned to Gary, Lindsey and Betty, "I'm sorry. Really, I am." She raced after Vinnie like a puppy after its owner.

The rest of happy hour for the NNJCC crew grew somber. No one really seemed to know what to say to one another and Rick, lost in his own thoughts, didn't even try to come up with conversation. He psyched himself up enough to perform, and though his song choices were more melancholy than usual, he managed to please the crowd anyway.

"What was that all about before, Rick?" Gary asked when they were sitting at the bar at the end of the night. Lindsey and Betty, along with most of The Tavern's patrons, had already cleared out.

Rick took another swig of his beer. "That man is vile."

"I agree, but it's not your place to tell him so."

"Somebody had to."

"But we hardly even know Lena. Couldn't you just ignore him?"

"No," Rick answered adamantly. "Did you see her face? He was humiliating her. She didn't deserve that. He doesn't deserve her. He's an asshole and she's….she's perfect," he whispered.

"Rick…she's getting married soon. Stay out of it."

"That's the thing. She can't marry him. He's no good for her."

"And I bet you think *you* are though."

Rick didn't respond to that. But he did know the answer.

The rest of the weekend Rick spent working on the old barn that sat behind his Craftsman style house on his four acres of property on White Lake Road in Sparta. He'd been renovating the barn so he'd have a sound proof room to record his music and a place big enough to put an air hockey table, a large screen TV, and a place to hang out. Rick started the project when he bought the house five years ago. He had a stable for his two horses, and he didn't really need a barn for its original intended use, so he thought he'd make himself a huge rec room. Besides, he enjoyed physical labor.

The lumbering was tedious, so by Sunday evening, an exhausted Rick retired to his favorite spot in the house – his recliner. As he relaxed in the dark, he lit a cigarette and attempted to reach his precious Angie from long ago...

Tonight....he was in luck....

"Let me walk you to church, Angie." He called after her while she hurried down the street, obviously late for Mass.

"Oh." She turned to see him pacing behind her several feet.

He reached her instantly. "I know you're running late, but I'd like to walk with you."

She smiled. Her eyes were golden-brown, her peaches 'n cream skin, flawless, and her chocolate-brown hair, sparkling in the early morning Sunday sun. *"Okay."* Her demure voice, music to his teenage ears.

He reached for her hand, and she placed it in his. They strolled to church hand in hand and remained that way all through Mass, stealing glances at each other while the priest celebrated Mass.

Afterward, they walked through town and shared an egg cream at the drugstore around the corner from Angie's house.

"So Angie, why do you always go to Sunday Mass by yourself?" asked a curious Richard.

She shrugged her frail shoulders. *"My mother doesn't even know I go. She sleeps late every morning. I bet she has probably never stepped foot in a church in her whole life."*

"So why do you go?"

"I guess I just need to hope there is someone out there looking after me."

That had been the first time he'd heard the desperation in her words and saw the sadness in her eyes. And that had been the first of many Sundays they would share a pew together at Mass.

Chapter Six

Monday morning came way too fast for Lena. Since she spent her whole weekend fretting over what her new co-workers were thinking about Vince, her stomach churned. She knew he would end up embarrassing her; he never did know how to present himself in public. That's why she hadn't invited him to go with her to The Tavern. But Vince, being the possessive and untrusting fellow he was, insisted on accompanying her. Now *she* had to endure the consequences of his actions. To his credit though, he had only been discourteous to Lena. Until he had seen disapproval written all over Rick's face, he had been good. But nothing gets him riled more than when someone passes judgment on him – and Rick did that by looking at Vince with disgust. Once Vince caught that, Lena knew things would go downhill much too fast.

She couldn't understand it though. Why would it bother Rick so much? He barely knew her; why would he feel the need to come to her defense like that? Not that it didn't make her feel just the tiny bit flattered. It certainly did. But it shouldn't have. What she should have been was mad, because he didn't mind his own business. How Vince treated Lena was her business, and if it didn't bother her, then it shouldn't have bothered anyone else.

But it *did* bother her. Every time Vince ridiculed Lena with his belittling words, he managed to diminish her self-esteem. She knew his abuse hurt her, but she couldn't tear herself away. His abuse hurt her both emotionally *and* physically. In public, he may only scold and scorn her, but in private, when his rage reached its highest limits, he imposed on her, physical pain. How many times had she had to come up with an excuse for a black eye or a bruised arm? Lena knew it was wrong, but she also knew Vince couldn't help himself, and she knew deep down that Vince never really *meant* to hurt her.

"Good Morning, Lena. Happy Monday." Lindsey beamed walking into Lena's cubicle. Lena began work by 7:50am, hoping to avoid everyone on the elevator. However, she couldn't avoid the co-workers that worked directly with her, and that included bubbly Lindsey. It amazed Lena that Lindsey's professional appearance at work misrepresented her personality. Friendly, bouncy, and anything *but* professional, Lindsey always managed to make Lena smile.

"Good Morning, Lindsey." Lena grinned. "Happy Monday, back."

"Hey, sorry about Rick butting in the other night. That must have been so uncomfortable for you."

Lena just shrugged.

"I don't know what possessed him to do that, he's usually so reserved and in control," Lindsey continued.

"Really?" asked a wide-eyed, Lena. "I just thought Rick was like that. You know, that he lashes out easily and….I don't know."

"No. He *never* lashes out. He's a pretty laid back guy."

"Good morning, Betty," Lena addressed the Engineering Secretary when she also entered Lena's cubicle.

Lindsey turned toward Betty. "Happy Monday, Bett. I was just telling Lena how uncharacteristic it was for Rick to get so worked up like he did Friday night."

"Yeah. I agree. Rick's not usually so impulsive, but…" Betty trailed off, pausing to look at Lena. "Honey, we really need to talk."

Lena averted her eyes and focused on her computer screen, not ready to hear what Betty had to say about Vince.

Betty shook her head. "I'm not done, sweetie. We *will* have that talk." Betty walked away.

"Sorry about that, Lena. I guess we should just get to work. How 'bout we go to lunch together today?" Lindsey asked.

Lena looked up at Lindsey and smiled. "Yeah. I'd like that." Grateful, Lena admired Lindsey's ability to lighten things up. Thanks to Lindsey's lunch invitation, Lena wasn't feeling as tense as she was earlier. The rest of the morning kind of flew by.

At lunch, Lindsey did most of the talking; though when Lena managed to get a few questions in, they were mostly about Rick. She tried not to seem too interested, but her curiosity to find out about the man who battled over her nobility, won. She found out that Rick Murphy did not date much. Though interested in woman, it appeared that Rick would only date someone for a while before losing interest. Jackie from the Customer Service department was one such unfortunate woman. Lindsey remembered last summer when Jackie came to her in tears, because Rick had told her that his heart belonged to someone else. Rick had been so wonderful to Jackie that she never saw it coming. Lindsey assured Lena that Rick had never been cruel; he just hadn't wanted to lead Jackie on when he couldn't find it in his heart to love her. Lena contemplated this and tried to fit it into her puzzling opinion of Rick. Was he old-fashioned, or just a jerk?

The rest of the week went by with a quiet intensity. Lena avoided the Engineering department, hoping to escape the well-meaning concern from her new friends. And every time Rick walked through the PR department and past her glass cubicle, Lena pretended to be engrossed in something on her desk or computer screen. She could not bring herself to come eye to eye with him. Besides, she had been looking forward to the weekend. On Saturday, she would take a trip down to Seaside Heights with her sister Katrina and her boyfriend Joe. And of course, Vince.

Lena awoke Saturday morning saddled with overwhelming emotion. Troubled by yet another dream weighing on her spirit, she began to believe they were images meant to communicate some underlying meaning – like fragments of a puzzle only she could piece together. But this puzzle was riddled with abuse. Why would she be dreaming of the same poor girl now being beaten by a man she called Timothy? Timothy who? Who was this girl?

Lena didn't have time to ponder last night's nightmare. Katrina, Joe and Vince would be here soon. Lena attempted to put aside her doubt and face today with a smile. Today would be a good day. It had to be. And like every day, she would block out the emotions she held behind her vibrant mask.

They took the scenic Garden State Parkway down to Seaside. Lena drove so Vince could drink his two-quart container of Gin and Tonic.

"Leen," Lena's baby sister by three years called from the back seat, cuddled close to Joe. "Why don't you put on some music?"

"Sure. I have Daughtry, Matchbox Twenty ....and oh....an old Holland CD."

"Ooh...Holland...please. It's so great that Cousin Mara is dating Tagg Holland, isn't it? Dating the lead singer of a famous rock band; how cool is that?"

"Jesus Christ, Lena. Sissy stuff?" Vince complained, not allowing Lena to respond to her sister's question. "No Metallica or Bullet For My Valentine?"

"Sorry, Vince," Lena said softly.

"Whatever."

Lena sang along to Holland's *She's My Only*, singing above the volume, when Vince found the need to deflate her.

"Oh for Crissake, just shut up already," he ordered.

Lena felt her face flush. She looked in the rearview mirror to see her sister's reaction. Katie and Joe seemed to pretend that they hadn't noticed. The rest of the ride, Lena didn't sing. For the rest of the ride, Lena remained silent and punctured; another pin pricking at her battered soul.

Barren of patrons in late April, the Seaside Heights boardwalk was very cool and windy. Lena loved the Jersey shore in the Spring. She loved the shore all year round, especially during its off-seasons. There weren't the crowds to distract from the beauty of the ocean or the wonder of the worn-out boards of the boardwalk. Lena never stopped to think about why she had loved the boardwalk and its over-used boards; the emptier it was, the more she felt like she belonged.

For the last few years, every time Lena would be down the shore, she'd get these visions of Seaside Heights that played out like an old-time movie. The carousel would revolve on its platform while the children whirled around the Wurlitzer organ on their ornately designed carousel horses. The children's cherubic faces and formal dress signaled an era almost a century old, yet these children were familiar…especially one particular wheelchair-bound little girl. The same children, the same boardwalk, and the same ill-treated woman repeatedly haunted her nightmares.

Today had been no different. Sitting across from the carousel on a bench on the boardwalk, Lena, Katrina and Joe enjoyed Kohr's ice cream, while Vince drank away his time at the bar. Lena's mind began to drift back in time.

Back on the carousel, the now familiar woman placed her handicapped little girl on the merry-go-round's bench, and the child blew her a kiss. The woman blew one back as she whispered the name Emmie. Emmie? She knew that name. Did she know that girl? Her mind told her she couldn't have known her; her heart told her she did.

Transported back to reality at the exact moment Vince came stumbling across the boards, Lena recognized his inebriated state. Vince must have noticed the annoyed look on her face, because suddenly he raged with defensive fire. She saw the fury in his eyes before she heard the ire in his words. "What's your problem, bitch?" He came at her and grabbed her shoulders. "You're looking at me like I killed someone, I'll give you something to be afraid of." He wasn't making any sense.

"Vince. No, I don't have a problem." Lena shook in fear, afraid of what he'd do. "Are you okay? You just looked like you were sick or something." She scrambled at anything to calm him quick, trying to avoid a drunken scene.

Lena trembled. Vince's hands moved from her shoulders to her wrists as he pinned her against the railing that separated the boardwalk from the beach. He closed in on her; he was nose to nose now. Then with all of his drunken force, he head-butted her. Lena's head whipped back, her knees buckled beneath her, and she went down.

Lena's vision went black for a second before everything became hazy. In the blur, she saw Joe pull Vince away from her and then fist him right in the face, knocking him to the ground. Joe hurried to help Katrina with Lena. Lena insisted she was okay, but Katrina wanted to get her home.

Kat and Joe helped her to the car, leaving Vince to fend for his drunken self.

Lena started crying. Mad at Vince for his behavior, she still felt sad for him. He didn't mean to be that way. She knew deep down that he hated himself for it.

"Joe," Lena finally said once they reached Route 35 heading out towards the Parkway. "Please turn around. We can't just leave him there."

Lena saw Katrina look at Joe and shrug.

"Okay, Leen, if that's what you want…but the guy's an ass. If it were up to me, I'd leave him here."

"Thanks, Joe."

After a very quiet drive home, Vince decided he was not worthy of Lena's love and demanded his engagement ring back. Knowing better than to argue with him, she slid the ring off her finger and slipped it into Vince's hand. After he calmed down, she thought, she'd talk some sense into him.

But did she really want to? Maybe she should seize this opportunity and let their engagement end. She hadn't been happy with Vince in a long time, and he did seem to get angrier each passing day.

Instead of deciding right this minute, though, Lena went to sleep. Maybe those nightmares she had were trying to tell her something. Maybe they'd talk to her tonight.

Chapter Seven

"Angie, sweetheart, you look beautiful," he said when he met her across the street; she, waiting for him to pick her up and walk her to Sunday morning Mass.

"Thank you." She blushed, as Rick threw his cigarette down on the ground and took her hand.

While strolling hand in hand on their way to church, he handed her a small gold box wrapped with a silken red ribbon. "What's this?" she questioned, her eyes wide in surprise.

"Open it."

She blushed again and let go of his hand to unwrap the gift. In it was a thin gold chain with a small heart locket that hung from it. "Oh my goodness, it's...beautiful, but..."

"Open it," again, he insisted.

Upon opening the delicate heart, she found a tiny picture of him pressed inside. He took the chain and locket from her hand and tenderly slipped it around her neck, holding the heart and placing it delicately over her chest. "Now...I will always be close to your heart..." He looked down at the ground and frowned. "No matter what."

"Oh...but don't you realize," she took his chin with her slender fingers and turned him to face her, "you are always close to my heart."

Rick bolted from his daydream when, instead of hammering the nail into a wooden slat, he pounded his own thumb with the tool. "Damn," he uttered, his cigarette falling out from its hold between his lips.

His entire weekend was spent renovating his barn. Rick had been disappointed all week, because he was unable to talk with Lena. He had felt bad about causing that scene with her boyfriend, and he'd wanted to apologize. But every time he made it a point to walk by her desk, she seemed to purposely avoid him. She was mad at him, as well she should be, but it just didn't sit right with him to not have apologized. Even though Vinnie, or whatever his name was, should be the one apologizing to Lena. So crass and vile, Vinnie did not deserve a girl as sweet as Lena.

Rick wondered what she was doing right now. Was she with that monster? Was she not? Was she thinking about Rick, like he was thinking about her? Since the day he ran into her in the parking lot, Lena sat at the forefront of his mind, occupying every other thought…and his heart. Since Lena's presence graced his existence, the empty space in his heart began filling with life. Now he just needed to find an opportunity to spend time with Lena so that he could win *her* heart.

On Monday morning, that opportunity presented itself. Dan Shoup was unable to attend the franchise meeting in Alpine with Rick. So in his place he sent his assistant Lena Giordano. Perfect. Rick would get to spend over an hour each way with her sitting merely inches away. Now hopefully he wouldn't mess up this God-sent turn of events.

Lena seemed somewhat surprised when Rick swung by her office to pick her up. "You ready, Lena?"

"Uh, yeah, uh sure…I guess." She turned to Dan and with a shaky voice asked, "Are you sure you want to send me? I'm new here. How could I possibly answer any of their questions?"

Confident in his response, Dan answered, "You'll be fine. Anything you don't know on our end, just tell them you'll get back to them tomorrow. Besides, today is the technical part of the meeting. Patrick will be doing most of the talking."

"Patrick?" Lena's puzzled expression made Rick and Dan chuckle.

"That'd be me, Lena," Rick answered from behind her.

"Oh. I thought…"

"I prefer Rick to Patrick or Pat. It suits me better.

"You two better get a move on," Dan interrupted, "meeting starts at 10:30."

Lena followed Rick to his Wrangler, now adorned with a roof and doors, where he opened the passenger side door to allow for her to step in.

"Thank you," she offered, as he closed the door after her.

"So Lena," Rick began, searching for something to talk about on the road. "What's your story?"

"My story?" She shook her head, "I don't have a story." She spoke softly, portraying an uneasiness about her present company.

Rick shrugged. "Everyone has a story, Lena."

Lena pursed her lips, unsure of what to say.

"Do I make you feel nervous?" Rick wanted to make her feel at ease, not anxious.

She uttered a small sound before answering, "No, I'm fine."

"I'm sorry," Rick began. "I just…I guess I feel pretty comfortable around you, that's all. I'm sorry if I came on too strong."

Lena shook her head again. "No, that's okay. You're fine." Lena hesitated momentarily and grinned. "So…. what's your story?" Her slow ricochet back at him seemed to please her, if her smug expression was any indication..

Rick snickered. "My story, huh? Well, where should I begin?"

"At the beginning," Lena joked. "How 'bout..." Lena put her finger to her chin and tapped it a few times. "Do you have a girlfriend?" Her flinch told Rick that she probably hadn't meant to say that. "I mean, do you have any siblings?" She recovered instantly.

Rick enjoyed sitting in the car with Lena. It made him smile to see her fluster so easily. "I am an only child and no." He shook his head. "I do not have a girlfriend." He took a sideways glance at her and grinned. "But it was hard not to notice that you have a boyfriend."

Lena put her head down. "Yeah, well."

Rick tried to watch the road, but Lena's expression looked so sad, he'd wanted to pull over and hold her. "Lena...about last week...at the bar. I am sorry that I got involved. It was definitely uncalled for...for what it's worth." He took his eyes off the road, a little too long, to allow for Lena to see his remorse. "I *am* sorry."

Lena rubbed the back of her neck with her hand. "Thank you."

"So...what's his name? Vinnie?"

"Vince."

Rick detected an edge to her voice. He couldn't tell if maybe there was a problem between her and Vince, or if the subject of Vince were off-limits to Rick. He figured he'd err on the side of caution and drop the subject. "Do *you* have any siblings?"

"Five. Four brothers, one sister. I'm the oldest."

"Wow. Six of you? I guess things never get boring at your house."

"Well, they do," another little sound emanated from Lena's throat, "because I live on my own now. It's quiet there…" Lena looked down at her lap. "It gets lonely…and boring. I go home a lot." Rick caught a smile on her face when he glanced over at her.

"You're a close family then?"

"Oh yes. I mean…we have our moments, but most of the time we really enjoy each other."

It surprised Rick to be so pleased to hear that. "Your parents? Are they happy people?" This felt important to ask.

"Oh sure. Mom's always walking around singing some old Bon Jovi song and Dad's always joking around."

"Are you being sarcastic?" Unsure of her tone, Rick needed to ask.

"No." Lena laughed. "I'm serious…of course, *they* never are."

"Serious, you mean?"

"Mm hmm. They're a lot of fun. I'm lucky to have them."

Rick felt something. Something very wrong. "Why are you sad then, Lena?"

"Sad? I'm *not* sad." Lena answered him much too quickly. "Why would you say that?" Lena's question had annoyance written all over it.

"I'm sorry. I didn't mean to offend you...looks like I'm getting off on the wrong foot here." Rick glanced at pretty little Lena. "Or sticking my foot in my mouth rather."

"It's okay," she mumbled.

Rick desperately wanted to win her over, but he rendered the exact opposite reaction. He was pushing her away. Out of the corner of his eye, he saw her staring out the passenger window and clasping her necklace like it would transport her out of his truck if she wished hard enough.

"Lena, I didn't mean to imply anything. I really am sorry. I must be making a terrible impression on you...can we...start over?"

Lena's gaze didn't stray from the road outside, but Rick saw a hint of a smile making its way onto her face. Good, he thought. Maybe all wasn't lost yet.

"My name is Rick. Yours?" He heard a chuckle. "What's that now? I think I missed it..."

"Lena." He heard another of her nervous laughters. "My name is Lena."

"Aaah. Nice to meet you Lena. Do you have any hobbies?"

"I like to bake...and crochet...I like to crochet." Lena's faced turned a flattering pale pink.

"Crochet, huh? That's an old-fashioned thing to do for someone so young."

"Yeah, I guess so..." Lena looked back down at her lap.

"It wasn't a put-down. Please don't think that. I..."

Lena didn't let him finish. "Rick. It's all right. I didn't take offense. I like crocheting. It relaxes me and I well, I found that I was good at it. Who knew?"

"I knew," Rick said to himself.

"What?"

Rick shook his head. "Uh...I mean...I knew, well, I've *heard* it's very relaxing. To crochet."

"Oh...yeah, it is."

Whew. "So...what do you like to bake?"

"Oh." Excited to answer, Lena's voice raised an octave. "I have this old cookbook that my grandmother won when she was a little girl. It has the best recipes in it. I've tried almost all of them, but I think the old-fashioned butter cookies are my favorite. I add different extracts to the recipe. I just love...I'm sorry. I'm rambling."

"No. No." Rick couldn't help but be filled with joy. He loved her passion. "You like baking. I get it."

The blush on her cheeks now turned a deeper pink, and Rick found that more endearing to him than her love of old traditions.

He would have kept driving just to keep listening to Lena talk, but they'd reached the Alpine municipal complex and it was already approaching 10:30am.

Chapter Eight

Lena felt relief during the meeting when she'd realized the only questions the citizens of Alpine had were technical ones. So about halfway through it, she'd relaxed and found herself captivated by Rick's knowledge and the ease at which he spoke to the crowd. Confident and composed, Rick emanated coolness. Yes...he was...cool. Lena laughed at her description of him. Since when had she ever considered a guy cool? This wasn't some leather-clad 1950s biker or something like that, but Rick possessed such a positive air about him that she couldn't think of a better word. Well, maybe she could, but...cool came to mind first.

Back in the Wrangler, and more nervous than before, Lena feared Rick would notice that, while they were in the meeting, she'd become even more fascinated by him. Would she be able to hide her attraction?

"So...that was an interesting meeting," Rick started.

"Yes." Lena wanted so badly to say something intelligent, but words were failing her.

"Are you hungry? Maybe we could grab some lunch before going back."

"Oh. Uh." This made Lena antsy. Sure, it was just lunch, but what would Vince think if he found out. He'd never understand that she and Rick were just co-workers. He'd flip. And besides, Lena's increasing infatuation with Rick would make it feel more like a date. "Do you think Dan will mind?" She feigned being more worried about her boss than her fiancé.

"Heck no. We always stop after one of these meetings. I'll call him and let him know."

"Oh…okay…I guess." Lena wanted to go to lunch with Rick. She really did. But she also knew that her attraction to him would only deepen. And she wasn't completely sure if spending more time with Rick would be the smartest thing to do.

Portobello's Restaurant was teeming with executives working through lunch. Yet even though the clientele were mostly professionals, Lena couldn't help but feel as if she were on a date. She had the butterflies in her stomach to thank for that. Poor Rick. Clueless to Lena's growing crush on him, he probably thought she was some timid creature. Well…in a way she was…but usually she'd have a bit more composure than the tangle of nerves she presented today.

"And for you, Miss?" The waiter, interrupting Lena's mulling, inquired about her menu choice.

"Oh...I'm sorry." Lena hadn't even focused on the words on the menu, she'd merely gazed at it. "Um, I guess...I'll have..." She glanced quickly at the menu, her eyes darting across it, but not settling on anything, so she opted for a safe standby. "I'll just have the pasta."

"Pasta?" the waiter mocked. "What *kind* of pasta?" he quipped. "We have about two dozen options."

Lena felt the warmth in her face and knew she'd turned some shade of crimson, adding to her humiliation. She grabbed on to her locket and fumbled with it near her face. "Oh, uh...just a marinara sauce, please."

The waiter abruptly took her menu and stormed away.

"I guess I made him mad." Lena, still fumbling with the locket, looked down at the table, afraid to meet Rick's eyes.

"Well, he shouldn't have gotten mad," Rick replied. "It's his job to be courteous. He wasn't doing his job."

Lena shrugged a shoulder and twisted in her seat, unable to speak yet from all of her awkwardness.

Rick must have realized it, because he tilted his gorgeous head to one side and gave her one of those pitying smiles, "Lena, sweetheart, don't worry about it. You were fine."

Sweetheart? Did he actually call her sweetheart? Okay, Lena had to shake this off. She was a twenty-five year old woman, not a fifteen year-old girl giddy with puppy love. "I know," she answered. "I'm good…. So…I've never been here." Her eyes slowly scanned the dining room. "It's nice."

"It is. We have a lot of our business lunches here, it's just…the place to go, I guess." Rick paused. "So, tell me about yourself. Where'd ya go to school?"

"You mean college?"

"Okay." Rick laughed.

Lena did too. "I went to Seton Hall."

"Impressive. Did you study PR?"

"Uh, no, not really. I mean, I'd taken some PR classes, but…I studied Television and Film Production."

"Wow. Cool." Rick knitted his brow. "Why are you here, then?"

"You mean at cable?"

"Yes."

"Um, not sure, really. It…" Lena shook her head. "It just didn't work out…in television, I guess."

Rick placed his fist under his chin and looked her right in the eyes, as if he were assessing something. He looked like he wanted to say something, but then sat back in his chair. "You're young. I'm sure it'll all work out."

She found his question puzzling, because Lena had the instinctual feeling that he had wanted to say something entirely different. What *wasn't* he saying?

"I'm not sure if I even want that anymore," Lena answered quietly.

"Well, what do you want?"

"I'm happy where I am, I guess."

"Really? Because it doesn't seem that way."

What? Why did he keep saying that? "Why do you keep saying that?" Irritated, Lena's voice rose in frustration.

Rick skewed up his face, looking baffled, and asked, "Keep saying what?"

Lena rolled her eyes toward the ceiling, then concentrated on fixing them on Rick's. "You keep saying that I'm not happy. I *am* happy," Lena scowled.

Rick chuckled. "You look it."

Lena pursed her lips again. This man infuriated her…when he wasn't turning her on. She repeatedly slid her locket from side to side across its chain. "I'm fine." Her response, clipped and defensive, she was mad at herself for letting this man's opinion bother her.

"I'm sure you are." He smiled. "Listen, Lena, my intention is *not* to anger you. I swear." Rick held up both his hands in surrender. "You may find it hard to believe," he continued, "but I'd really like to be your friend." He reached for her hand across the table.

The fiery warmth of his hand on hers sent a current through her so intense, she felt her heart burning beneath her chest. She felt the electricity. Of course, the responsible thing for an engaged woman to do would be to pull away, but Lena found this simple task extremely difficult. After a long couple of seconds, she slowly slid her hand from his and placed it on her lap. His emerald eyes were potent magnets, gripping at her soul, as he stared intensely into her eyes. Because of the impact his gaze had on her, she had to force herself to look away. She opted instead to look at her water glass. Fortunately, the waiter had broken the awkward silence by serving their meals.

"I like your heart," Rick decided to say at the same moment Lena was putting a forkful of pasta in her mouth.

"Hmm?" Lena attempted to respond with as much couth as someone with a mouthful of food could muster.

"Your heart." Rick pointed a finger at the spot just below her neck. "Your necklace."

"Oh." Lena cupped her hand around the locket again and slid it across the chain a few times. "Thank you."

"It looks old."

"It is." Lena continued on with her meal.

"Okay." Rick seemed uncomfortable now. "I guess you're still agitated with me. Why don't we just finish our lunch and get going?"

Lena felt bad now. She didn't mean to alienate Rick; she just didn't want to explain her perpetual sadness. How could he tell she was unhappy anyway? Usually so careful to hide her weariness, Lena couldn't understand how this beautiful, wondrous man could see right through her. He caught a glimpse of her soul, and she wasn't sure how to pull the shades down to keep him from peering in.

Chapter Nine

At home, Lena changed into her sweats and restlessly waited for Vince to come over. She wondered if he would give her the ring back. She kind of hoped he wouldn't. It'd make things so much easier if he were to break things off. If he didn't, then she'd be stuck with having to make that decision herself. She'd also been afraid Vince would ask her about her day, and she'd have to divulge that she went to lunch with another man. Vince would never understand that Rick was just a co-worker. Especially since Lena's temperature raised a few degrees every time she was near Rick. Sometimes just thinking about him made her feel warm all over. Could Vince know this? Lena sure hoped not; she couldn't imagine what Vince would do if he realized she was attracted to another man. Certain his stormy temper would take over, her body trembled with the thought.

All her worrying had been for naught. Vince wasn't concerned with Lena's day, her thoughts, *or* the engagement. He showed up, handed her the ring, and began his yelling.

"Hurry up, Lena. I need you to drive," he roared. "I'm out of weed."

His one concern this evening? The need to get more marijuana. Unbelievable. "Drive? You want me to drive you to Paterson so you can buy drugs?" A flabbergasted Lena asked as she slipped the ring back on her finger, disappointed that she lost a convenient opportunity to end their engagement.

"Geez, Lena, you make it sound like a crime."

"*It is a crime.* Last I checked, pot was still illegal," she declared. She did not like this. She already disliked being around him while he smoked it, did she need to be part of the purchasing of it as well? "I'm not comfortable with…"

"Shut it, Lena, and get in your car."

"Vince, I don't want to…"

"Get in," he growled and then grabbing hold of her arm, shoved her against the car, opened the door and pushed her in. "Here are your damn keys." He threw them on her lap and got in on the passenger's side.

This part of Paterson unfamiliar to Lena, her body shivered in fear. The steep hill they descended could have actually been the road that led to the gates of Hell. As far as Lena was concerned, this *was* Hell. At the very bottom of the hill were 'The Projects.' Not 'The Projects' that Vince took her to last time, filled with signs of family life – kids riding their bikes, mothers sitting on their front steps, and laundry hanging from the clothes lines. No. These 'Projects' held despair and hopelessness. Young adults destitute of love. Boys carrying guns and weapons. Teenagers having sex in the alleys. This was out of Lena's comfort zone, and at this very moment she wished she could have stood up to Vince and demanded he go buy his drugs alone.

Vince had her stop at a group of guys who seemed to be expecting him. One of them approached Vince, showed him a little Ziploc baggie, and with little communication and a simple exchange of goods, Vince's drug interaction was complete. Vince instructed Lena to make two right-hand turns, and they now ascended the street that brought them back to civilization.

Disgusted with herself for allowing her resolve to crumble and letting Vince to strong-arm her into his illegal jaunt, her heart squealed in pain. She knew right from wrong, and this was wrong. Very wrong. Though she found it difficult to say no to Vince, saying yes all the time was getting old. She wanted to tell him no, damn-it. She wanted to tell him to 'shove-it' sometimes. What she wanted…was out of this relationship.

How could she not have seen it before? Lena did not belong with Vince. Not at all,…but how would she convey that to him? He…he'd go insane when she showed up late to his house. What would he do when she told him she wanted to break off their engagement? He would fly off the handle. He'd hurt her. Of that, she was certain. Darn, why couldn't he have just kept the ring? Why couldn't she just not have taken it back? It should have been so easy to say 'you know what, Vince? Keep it.' But no, she took the ring back without saying a word, in true Lena fashion. Being a coward would keep her stuck in this situation forever…unless she could find the strength to stand up to him. She needed to find that strength. Determined to find it, she made a promise to herself to do so.

Instead of agonizing over her recent revelation to become a stronger person, she decided to drop Vince at his car and go up to her apartment to sleep. Too tired to think, too tired to breathe, she must have passed out immediately, because soon she had propelled into another nightmare – more unsettling, more violent than the others. *A horrid man in a suit was striking her across the face repetitively. In her arms, a baby. At her ankle, a toddler. Another child, crying in the corner, was begging the man to stop hurting his mama.*

Lena knew she was dreaming and managed to force herself out of her nightmare. Though just a dream, it felt so real. Would this be her future with Vince? Is this what she had waiting for her if she went through with the marriage?

But the man? It wasn't Vince.

Who was it?

And why was she seeing him in her dreams?

Chapter Ten

After an entire night of chiding himself for coming on too strong with Lena, Rick found himself fretful and anxious on Tuesday morning. He wanted to apologize once again for his offensive accusation that Lena was an unhappy soul. Not that he'd said so in so many words, but he got the feeling that on some level, that's what Lena had heard.

His heart ached for her, and he knew it should be utterly ridiculous for someone he just met to have that kind of effect on him, but he couldn't help himself. He'd been waiting for her all his life. She may not have reciprocated his feelings, but he hoped in time she would.

Rick was busy filling out his monthly maintenance report, so he hadn't seen Lena pass by his office, but the lingering scent of her perfume had revealed her presence. He immediately set his work aside and rushed to the doorway. There she stood, in Betty's cubicle across the hall. She was stunning. And as he took in all of her five-foot beauty through Betty's plexi-glass walls, he observed her in slow motion, as if he were watching her on film. He breathed in the fragrance that still wafted in the air, while he watched her converse with his co-worker. Lena's eyelashes were like little butterflies batting at her cheekbones every time she laughed; the sound of her sweet voice resonating as music to his ears.

In the midst of Rick's reveling, Lena turned and caught him staring. He didn't look away. He *wouldn't* look away. Her eyes met his, and for a few brief moments they spoke without saying a word. His soul spoke of a love eternal, while hers communicated a love unknown. He could read it on her face. She'd remembered him. For one short instant, he saw recognition in her eyes.

Now if he could only help her to hold on to that discovery.

****

Her breath caught the moment her eyes met with his. For a fraction of a second, she saw a man so familiar that a flicker of a memory flitted through her mind. But just as sudden as it came into view, it had disappeared. Although her glimmer of something unexplained had lasted for one fleeting moment, its impact was powerful. She could not tear her gaze from the man that stood across the hall. She'd just met Rick Murphy; she couldn't have known him before. Her imagination. It had to be. Her mind did have a habit of playing tricks on her. But why was his gaze so intense? And why was her heart beating so fast?

"Lena." Prompted from the magnetic force of Rick's emerald-green eyes by his velvety-smooth voice, Lena heard Rick say, "When you're finished with Betty, would you mind seeing me in my office?"

"Uh. Uh-hum." Her throat needed clearing from her recent flash of paralysis.

While Betty recounted the customer complaint that Lena had inquired about before the sight of Rick Murphy had taken her breath away, Lena tried fruitlessly to recapture the image she held for a mere twinkling. What did Rick have to do with her unexplained whisper of a memory? And how was he able to arouse in her such excitement? Her insides were jumbled and jumpy. He intrigued her, yet he frightened her. Rick Murphy brought to the surface, an awareness that, in Lena, lay dormant for many years. Possibly a lifetime.

A virtual stranger, Rick Murphy was no one to Lena Giordano. So why did she have the glaring suspicion that she'd met him before?

Rick had been seated at his desk when Lena reluctantly walked into his office. Steeling herself for whatever he needed from her, she stood rigid and uncomfortable, feeling the fool when her entrance caused him to snicker.

"Lena." His smile held a slight laugh, but he actually stood from his seat to welcome her in. Who did that anymore? "I wanted to give you the technical forms for Alpine," he continued. "They're complete and ready to be submitted to the OCTV."

The OCTV? The Office of Cable Television? *That's* all he wanted? After that seemingly significant moment they shared from across the hall, all he wanted was to give her a flippin' technical form? "Oh. Um. Ok. Thank you." A chagrined Lena hastily took the forms from Rick, only to have them slip from her hand, scattering them across the floor. Scuttling down to gather the paper, Lena and Rick collided. Thunder bolted and lightning struck when Rick's hand brushed Lena's, and he left it there. Her gaze caught his, and her blood pulsed strong, rushing through her veins when he stared into her eyes. "Lena," he rasped.

Her breath, an involuntary inhale. Their gaze,... frozen.

"Lena." He attempted a stronger proclamation this time. "Would you…like to get a slice of pizza with me for lunch…today?"

Another breath caught in Lena's throat. Oh my goodness. Yes. She'd love to. But…she couldn't. "Um…I…uh…no, thank you. I'm sorry," she regretfully declined.

And just like that, he stood from his crouched position, leaving her momentarily slinking beneath him.

"Okay." He held out a hand to help her up. "Maybe some other time."

"Sure." She swung around and left his office, taking a moment in the hall to gauge what had just happened.

What was it about Rick that made her whole world turn upside down? The potency behind his gaze served as a strong poison to a girl engaged to someone else. Though never particularly satisfied with Vince in her life, she had made the commitment, and until recently, was set to honor it. But now…how could she…when all she could think about was Rick Murphy?

Chapter Eleven

"What the hell's your problem, Lena?"

Lena stumbled backwards, almost falling down the stairs, when she'd unlocked the door to her apartment and Vince was already inside. "Vince. What are you *doing* here?"

"Don't change the subject, Lena. What's your problem? You're in another world lately."

"Vince, what are you talking about?" Sidestepping him to put her purse on the table by her front door, Lena couldn't avoid his shoving her against the wall. He pinned her to it by grasping her wrists. "Vince, please. Let me go."

"Tell me what's going on?" he demanded.

"Nothing's going…I don't even know what you're talking a…"

"Shut it," he growled, pulling her away from the wall and pushing her across the room.

"Vince. Why?" Lena cried, before he picked her up and threw her flying through the air.

But he didn't let her finish. "You're screwin' somebody else, aren't you?"

"What? No. Vince. Where'd you get that idea?" Lena scrambled to get to her feet, but Vince caught her and shoved her back against the wall.

"You can't fool me, Lena. Your mind's somewhere else and if it ain't on me, it's gotta be on some effin' other guy."

This was true. She definitely had her mind on someone else, but how in the world could Vince have known that? Darn. His intuitiveness scared her, but he had it all wrong. How could she convince him? "Vince. No. Not at all. Please," she begged.

But he didn't care what she had to say. He just concerned himself with his warped view of reality. If he already had it in his mind that Lena had spent time with another man, then nothing she could say could stop those thoughts. "You're a bitch. Y'know that?"

Lena tried to propel herself forward to loosen Vince's hold on her, but instead, it gave him more leverage to grab her around the waist and throw her onto the couch. "You're mine baby? Then prove it," he said angrily, while tearing her dress right off her body.

"Vince. No. Not tonight. Please. Another time, okay?" Lena implored, pleading for him to get off of her. He would not.

She tried to fight him off, but he used his hand and slapped her in the face. Her head shot in the direction he hit. Twisting to get herself out from under him, she failed. He punched her on the other cheek, causing her defeat. The mixture of black and colored spots entered her vision. He must have used all his might in his fist. She felt her consciousness slipping away. He tore off her tights and plunged himself deep inside her, bringing her back to her senses as she screamed out in pain. Releasing himself, he pulled out, pulled up his pants and took off with nary a glance back. Lena was left prostrate…violated and shaken.

Trembling with dismay and momentarily paralyzed, Lena remained curled up in the fetal position, where she stayed until the sun hinted at dawn through the gaps in the blinds.

Morning brought with its new day, the stark realization that Lena was engaged to a merciless and soulless human being.

****

Lena's absence from work the past three days wasn't boding well in Rick's mind. He had the discerning feeling she was not sick. In fact, the nagging ache in his chest signaled a much worse fate. He needed to rescue her.

It took him about fifteen minutes to get to Haledon after hounding the Personnel department for Lena's address. He saw her car parked in the apartment complex's parking lot. Number 14. He had the right place. Though his nerves were standing on end, he had to do this, had to help her. Without further thought, he rang the bell.

And waited.

After five long minutes of ringing the bell, he heard footsteps plodding down the stairs.

Unprepared for what he saw in front of him when the door crept open, Rick gasped. The eyes peeking through the crack were of someone so familiar, his knees nearly buckled beneath him. This could not be happening again. It had to be better this time. Destiny could not be this cruel a second time around.

He needed to get a grip. "Lena," he whispered.

She cleared her throat, then let out something inaudible.

"Lena. Let me in."

She shook her head. "I'm sorry." But he barely heard her. Her soft voice sounded as if it hadn't been used in days.

"Please, Lena. I want to help."

She shook her head again and pushed the door to shut it, but Rick used his hand to keep it from closing. "Lena." His voice unfaltering, he gently nudged the door open and stepped inside. Exposed on one side of her cheek was a faded bruise. Someone had hit her.

"No. No. Nonononono. Leave me alone," Lena pleaded and then broke down. Banging her hands against his chest and pushing him back, she screamed,. "Get out, get out. Out."

Lena's swollen eyes begged for tears, but it looked as if she'd been crying for so long that there were no more tears to cry.

"Sweetheart, it's okay," Rick whispered, grabbing hold of her and pressing her head to his chest. He slid his hand over her tangled hair and breathed, "Shhh. It's okay." He continued to stroke her hair. "It's okay."

The gasps of breath Lena was offering in response proved she had been crying for far too long. Rick closed the door behind him and picked her up, cradling her in his arms to carry her up the stairs. He shoved blankets and used tissues aside and sat her down on the couch. Kneeling on the floor before her, he took her hands. "What happened?" was all he whispered, but all she needed to hear to allow herself to fall into his arms.

"I can't." The tears finally released. And released. And released.

"Then at least let me dry your eyes." Cupping her face in his hands, his thumbs wiped the tears that escaped her eyes.

Rick's own eyes began to tear as he stared into her crestfallen brown eyes. He thought he heard a slight chuckle between her sobs. "What?"

"Why are *you* …crying?" She laughed and cried simultaneously.

"When *your* heart breaks, mine absorbs the pain."

Now Lena looked befuddled. "But…you hardly even know me."

Rick took his eyes off of her momentarily to look down, then he returned his attention to her sad chocolate eyes. He wanted to tell her. But now was not the time. So he simply said, "I'd like to know you better." Which was the truth.

Lena shook her head. "Why? Why would you want to get to know *me*? I'm so…messed up."

"Well, I think you are perfect." He continued to caress her cheek with his thumb.

She averted her eyes and grew silent. But Rick saw her chest rise less noticeably and her breathing become less labored. She was calming down, accepting his friendship. That was a start.

"Lena, can I make you a cup of tea or something?" Rick broke the slight awkwardness of the moment.

"Oh. Sure. I'll get it though."

Lena got up and Rick took her hand. "Show me the way."

In the kitchen, Rick watched Lena fumble through the cabinets, searching for something. "Lena, do you not drink tea?" he asked, noticing the tons of single-serve coffee cups on the counter.

"Um, well, not really."

"Let me guess," Rick signaled to the big Keurig coffee machine sitting on the counter. "You like coffee," he stated, not asked.

"Mm-hmm." She smiled.

"Then why on Earth would you accept a cup of tea from me?"

She shrugged. "Because you offered."

"Oh, my dear. You *are* something. Show me how this thing works and I'll make you a cup of coffee."

Lena offered a slight giggle and silently walked him through her single-serve coffee making process. He made a second cup on his own.

"I like your apartment," Rick said, as he led them back into the living room and onto the couch.

"Thank you."

"Have you had it long?"

"Um…yes…no."

"Okay?" He wondered.

Lena chuckled again and Rick's heart warmed at the sound of her.

"My grandfather owns it. He lets me live here…for free."

"Ooh. Very nice."

Lena raised a shoulder, then dropped it. "I guess."

"Did you grow up in this town?"

"Yup. Been here all my life."

"Oh. Where do your parents live?"

"Right up the street on Belmont…next to Frank's Liquors."

"Right. I passed that on the way here. The liquor store? You're right next door?"

Lena smiled. "Yeah, my dad owns the store. Convenient, right?"

"Mmm." Rick looked at her and raised his hand to her tender cheek. "Did you put anything on this?"

"Mmm. A couple days ago. Ice."

"Did anyone get a look at it? Your nose could be broken."

Lena's head came down, suddenly looking ashamed all over again.

"Lena. Who did this?"

"Why are you here, Rick?" she asked, ignoring his question.

Rick put his cup down on the coffee table, then reached for Lena's mug and placed it next to his. He maneuvered closer to her, lacing his fingers with hers. "I knew something was terribly wrong." He caressed her cheek. "And now I have proof."

Lena closed her eyes and shook her head. "But…how? How did you know that?"

"Call it a sixth sense. Lena, I could just…feel it."

"But…how?"

Words caught in his throat. What could he tell her that wouldn't scare her away? This time *he* shrugged. "I just…know," he intimated, then paused a few seconds. "Do you wanna talk about it?"

Lena shook her head. "Not yet," she said in a quiet whisper.

"Well, did you at least talk with your parents?"

Lena's head shot up, and eyes wide, she blurted, "No. No I can't," and tapered off.

Rick covered both her hands inside his. "Oh, Lena. You can't keep this in. Whatever it is, whoever did this…and I'm sure I can guess… you can't *not* tell someone. And this can't happen again."

Lena removed her hands from Rick and slumped her head into them, leaning her elbows on her legs. Rick let her cry it out again while he caressed her heaving back.

He wanted to rescue her from her troubles, but since she wouldn't allow it, he'd have to settle for silently comforting her while she worked this out in her head.

But he couldn't sit idly by and watch her hurting. He couldn't let her down again. This time…he wouldn't let her down.

Chapter Twelve

Lena drifted off to sleep that evening a little easier, thanks to Rick's visit that afternoon. Even her dreams had a less haunting nature to them than usual. As a matter of fact, Lena awoke with a smile on her face. During the night, in her other world, she walked hand in hand with Rick down the perfect main street village. It was almost like a scene from an old movie. A smile was plastered on her face as she fussed with her gold heart locket, no longer broken.

Lena couldn't remember many other details of the dream, but she certainly had recalled her emotions. Happy and suddenly carefree, she wanted to bottle up those feelings, because she knew they had been few and far between, both in her fictional dream and in her all too real life.

Her problems with Vince hadn't disappeared, but she had managed to avoid him since that dreadful night, claiming to him that she had the flu, and he needed to stay away so he wouldn't catch it as well. Her mother seemed to accept her excuse as well, but each time her mom attempted to visit or bring her chicken soup, Lena feigned sleepiness and averted the much-needed visits. Lena didn't have the heart to tell her mother what Vince had done. It would kill her. Yet Lena really needed the comfort of her mother's hugs...and her chicken soup.

Lena woke ready to return to work. Make-up could hide the faded redness on her cheek, and Rick had put the smile back on her face. It wasn't deep enough to reach her heart, but it was close. Looking forward to seeing Rick at work, she pushed thoughts of Vince aside for the day. If only it were that easy to push him away for real.

The whole day went by in an instant. Lena had so much work to catch up on that she'd worked through lunch. Already five o'clock, she hadn't even had the chance to walk by Rick's office and thank him for sitting with her yesterday. She had barely talked, yet he stayed with her...even while she napped...on his lap. She hadn't remembered falling asleep, but she woke up, her head on his lap, the back of his fingers stroking her cheek. For a brief while, Lena felt as if someone had unlocked the door to her heart and returned her home. She couldn't explain it, but at that very moment, she felt that her whole life she had been waiting for Rick Murphy to welcome her home.

Of course, reality hit like a ton of bricks and recent events flashed back into her mind. Rick had been the indirect cause of Vince's anger four nights ago. Lena didn't know how Vince had guessed it. She assumed she had been so careful with her thoughts, but he intuited them anyway. Today was not about Vince though. Thoughts about Vince would be pushed aside. Today she wanted to thank Rick. She only hoped it hadn't been too late.

After today's assignments were complete, and her desk, cleared, Lena ventured down to Rick's office trying to ignore the butterflies fluttering in her stomach. When she entered, he seemed to be expecting her. Not that he expected any gratitude, more like he had wished for her and here she was. His smile, warm and genuine, he stood and walked over to greet her.

"Lena." Rick put a hand on the small of her back, causing another swift rush of flutters. "Sit down. I heard you were back today."

"Oh." Then why didn't he walk by like he usually did, she thought?

"I figured you had a lot of work to catch up on," he said, uncannily answering her thoughts.

"Mmm. That's an understatement."

"How ya feeling today? Any better?" The deep concern on his face flattered Lena. But for the life of her, she couldn't understand why he cared. Nor could she understand the intensity of her own feelings toward him.

"I'm better. Thank you." She took a deep breath and fuddled with the broken locket that hung around her neck. "Rick, thank you so much for yesterday. I'm not sure why you showed up…but…I'm really glad you did." It took all Lena's mental energy not to jump up and hug him. Boy she wanted to, but she was still engaged to Vince. Though she knew she had to break that commitment soon, she hadn't yet, and initiating any physical contact with Rick wouldn't be prudent.

"Well, I'm glad I did also," Rick assured her. "I wish I could do more, love, but…when you're ready…I'm here."

The tingles in her stomach were distracting, and Lena sighed before saying, "Thank you, Rick." He'd called her love. Her heart became heavy once again. She could feel the weight crushing her chest. All of a sudden, she wanted to cry. With all her might, she tried to prolong the tears. Her throat tightened where the lump was forming, and her eyes widened to let the air dry the tears before they sprung. Words were going to fail her, so she stood and walked out. From behind her, she could feel Rick watching her rip through the hallway in a hurry to leave work…before anyone saw her break down.

In her car, she hastened to leave the parking lot. Once she was on the road, she allowed the tears that swelled up in her eyes to flood down her face. She wanted Rick so much. But she couldn't have him. Not when she was still tethered to Vince. And she knew it'd be a difficult task to sever that link. His family was too big...too important to allow anything disparaging to be said about them. Who would believe her when she finally revealed the horrid truth about Vince Battaglia? *Her* family of course, but *his* family? The town?

Lena knew the Giordanos were just as prominent a family in the town as the Battaglias, but they had much more money to offer the town to keep any gossip at bay. How was she going to do this? When was she going to do this? It had to be soon. It had to be yesterday.

Lena stopped by her parents' house on the way home from work. She loved walking into her childhood home. Its Victorian charm was comforting in its prim and proper way, but the coziness and love that her mother Jules put into it added warmth and intimacy. Jules loved her large family, and it showed in everything she did for them. Even the coffee she perked over the gas stove had the aroma of love – its smokey, yet full-bodied taste shouted, 'Come. Sip me. Stay awhile.' Although it lacked the convenience of Lena's Keurig, her mother's coffee trumped convenience in smell, taste and enjoyment. Just like coming home to Mom and Dad trumped going home to her empty apartment.

What had she been thinking moving out on her own? She was much happier here at home. Big deal if she were twenty-five and still living at home. Many people were doing that now as a result of the poor economy. Why had she been in such a rush to leave?

Vince was why she was in such a hurry to move out. He kept insisting that if she wouldn't move in with him, she should at least have her own place for him to stay over. Ironically, she'd never let him stay the night anyway. It just never felt right.

Now here she lived in her own apartment, more unhappy than ever.

"Lena, sweetheart," Jules hailed when she saw her daughter in the kitchen doorway. "I'm so happy you're here. How are you feeling? Any better?"

"Yeah, Mom, I'm better." Lena slowly pulled out one of the high-back Victorian-style kitchen chairs and sat down, leaning her head in her hand.

Jules must have caught Lena's silent sigh, because after preparing her daughter a cup of coffee, she sat it in front of her, sat down next to her, and placed both her hands over Lena's free hand. "Sweetie. What's the matter? Why are you so sad?"

Lena didn't even try to stop this round of tears. She allowed them all to flow, like a weakened dam succumbing to the weight of the water. Yet, although the tears could freely tumble, the words would not. They remained prisoners in her mind, unable to free themselves from the torment.

"Lena, honey, what?" Jules empathized, unable to get hold of her own emotions while her daughter broke down in front of her.

Lena just shook her head, still leaning on her hand. Her breathing came out in clips. Little hiccups between cries.

"Baby... is it Vince?"

Still cradling her head, Lena nodded.

"Did he cheat on you?"

She shook her head.

"Was he fresh?"

A nod.

"Oh sweetie. What'd he say?"

What could Lena say? 'Mom. He raped me. Twice.' No. She couldn't tell her mom that now. That bridge should have been crossed a year ago, the first time Vince stole her innocence. How 'bout, 'Mom. He beats me. Regularly.' No. Another bridge untouched. What was left? Another truth. "Mom," she cried into her hand, still being used as a support. "I don't want to get married." She finally dropped her hand and looked at her mother. "Not now. Not to Vince."

"You are young yet," her mom validated. "I never did think you were ready."

Lena wiped her eyes. "Really, Mom? It's okay to break it off?" Lena asked, with just the tiniest hint of hope.

"Of course, Lena. Your father and I would never want you to do anything you're not ready for. *Especially* marriage."

Jules' reassuring support was like a beacon in the night. Lena finally could see happiness up ahead.

But how would she tell Vince? It wouldn't be easy. And she most definitely could not do it alone.

"Mom. Could you and Daddy help me tell Vince and his parents? I...really don't want to do it alone."

"Of course. Now," Jules got up and went to the stove, "how 'bout some pot roast?"

Suddenly, Lena felt famished. "Okay. I love your pot roast." Lena got herself a plate and brought it to her mom. "Where is everybody? I mean...Daddy's working, but what about Katrina and the boys?"

"Katrina's at Joe's house, Francis is working and Antonio is at school. Nicky and Christopher are with Daddy. Wrestling practice. Dad's not working tonight."

"Oh."

"They should be home soon. Why don't you stay here tonight? You know your room upstairs is still yours."

Lena liked that idea. "Yeah. I will. I still have half my clothes here, so I don't even need to go get anything."

"Great." Jules was perfect. Lena was so grateful that she had her for a mother.

Tomorrow, she'd be unengaged.

And finally free from Vince Battaglia.

Chapter Thirteen

Vince bolted through the Giordano's front door, crashing it into the bottom step of the staircase. "Lena," he bellowed.

Jules came running to the door, Christopher following. Lena stood in the kitchen doorway, afraid to move forward.

"What's your problem, Vince? You don't bust in our house like that," fifteen-year-old Christopher warned.

"Christopher." Jules put her hand on his shoulder. "Now, Vince. What's got you so upset that you need to crash through our front door without knocking?"

"Lena's avoiding me. I wanna know why," he commanded.

"Vince. She's been sick. Today was her first day out, and I asked her to stay here for the night."

"What'd she tell you?" Vince once again demanded an answer. Lena peered out from behind the half-wall that blocked her from Vince's sight.

"Lena," he howled. "What'd you tell 'em?"

"Nothing, Vince," Lena said quietly, wishing he would just go away. "Nothing. I...I."

Jules put her hand up to stop Lena from finishing her sentence. "Vince, come in the kitchen, now. C'mon. I'll get you a cup of coffee. We'll sit," Jules turned to Christopher, "Go get your father. He's upstairs."

Christopher two-stepped the staircase. Vince followed Jules and Lena into the kitchen.

Fortunately, when Frank came home earlier, Lena had informed her father of her decision to break up with Vince. Frank's only apprehension was his concern for the Battaglias. He knew in a large, estimable family like theirs, a broken engagement would definitely be public fodder, and he would never want to discredit their reputation. But in the end, it was Frank's daughter's well-being that mattered above all else. He gave his support and promised to help her through it.

Lena's father Frank entered the room as he entered every room, commanding respect by his mere presence – a man of short stature yet great power, the effect of holding world powerlifting records for the past two decades.

Aggravated and tense already, Vince sat rigid when the older man sat down across from him. His chest stuck out like a cave man ready for a fight.

Frank sat calm and easy, sipping the coffee his wife offered. "Now Vince." Frank's even tone was meant to not offend an already edgy Vince. "Lena came to me tonight with a request."

Lena's trembles were apparent to everyone, as her bouncing foot actually caused the table to shake. The locket around her neck was in its usual place, enveloped in her palm and close to her heart. Disappointed in herself for not breaking up with Vince herself, she closed her eyes and hung her head low. He scared her. If she had tried to tell him herself, the words would have never come out.

"And what request would that be, sir?" Vince's question held disdain.

"She's decided she's not ready to get married."

Slamming his hands on the table and jumping to his feet, Vince snarled, "No. She does not get to make that decision."

Never ashamed of standing almost a head shorter than most men, Frank also stood and advanced closer to Vince. "Yes, Vince, I'm afraid she does have the right, as would you, if you felt that way."

The wrath behind Vince's eyes, though fearful, caused a swell of sympathy in Lena's heart. She felt terrible about hurting Vince's feelings. Despite his gruff and barbarous ways, Lena had a soft spot for Vince, realizing that he really believed he was entitled to his ill-mannered ways. His parents had always been so tied up in business and society events that Vince had always been an afterthought. Lena couldn't help but empathize with him. Though her childhood had been full of her parents' attention, something deep inside of her felt the pain of neglect.

But then Vince's piercing glare, now directed at her, had punctured that soft spot for him, bringing her back to the real reason she couldn't marry Vince. His grueling brutality could eventually get her killed…literally. Lena averted her eyes from his stare but managed a timid, "I'm sorry."

Without glancing at him, his glower still held enough rage that she could almost imagine the heat of his blood boiling beneath his skin. Thankfully, in the next instant she heard his footsteps striding through the house, followed by the front door slamming behind him.

Lena collapsed to the floor.

"Oh my goodness! Frank," Jules cried.

Frank kneeled next to his daughter. "Call 911," he directed to Christopher. "Jules, go get my smelling salts from my first aid case. It's in my wrestling bag."

Jules hastily searched Frank's black duffel bag and retrieved the smelling salts. "Here." She handed it to Frank.

"Open it first, Jul." Frank had one hand under Lena's head, leaving only one free hand. He took the open package from Jules and held it beneath Lena's nose.

"Uggh, ewww." Lena groaned but then closed her eyes again.

Frank kept waving the salts under her nose. "C'mon, Leen. Get up," Frank pleaded.

"Eww. Uggh." Lena shook her head. "Hmmm," she mumbled. The room was hazy, but soon her father came into focus. After a couple of seconds, Lena became wide-eyed, not liking the smell of the salts at all.

"Lena, what happened?" Jules asked.

"I don't know…I…I got lightheaded."

Christopher walked in just then with the paramedics, who took Lena's vitals, fed her some Coke with added table sugar, and told her not to drive for at least two hours. The paramedics were in and out within twenty minutes time and chalked it up to a fainting spell. Then they suggested she see a doctor to determine its cause.

Chapter Fourteen

Monday morning, Rick felt the need to talk with Lena before going to his office. After thinking about her all weekend, he had decided to pursue her friendship more aggressively. No longer able to accept the sadness that lurked behind her eyes, his intention was to replace her sorrowful heart with a heart filled with joy, if it were the last thing on Earth he would ever do.

She was busy writing at her desk when Rick stopped cold in his tracks. There she was, sitting behind the glass cubicle. Beautiful...vulnerable...sad. It may not have been apparent to most, but to Rick...it was as clear as the blue sky on a tragic day. Lena's beauty overwhelmed by the wounds that ran deep inside her. She could not hide that from him.

But Rick had a reason for being here. To mend those wounds.

He lifted his feet from the floor and approached the fair maiden in distress.

"Lena." She looked up from her writing pad and smiled. "How are you, Miss?"

Lena giggled. "Hi, Rick."

He sauntered nearer to her desk and stopped, fumbling with the keys in his coat pocket. "Lena." Rick paused to collect his thoughts, even though he'd gone over it at least a hundred times. "There's this park down the road. Sunnybank. I go there sometimes to think. Well..." He wanted to ask her to join him there for lunch, but he was sure she would object to driving there together. "Um, could you meet me there today? About one?" He noticed her eyes widen, but he continued his spiel anyway. "I packed a picnic lunch in the hopes that you would join me," he questioned, bracing himself for another rejection.

"Okay."

"Wait. What?" Did he hear her correctly?

Lena smiled. "I said okay."

Left speechless, Rick wanted to walk up to her and hug her...then thank her for agreeing to see him today.

She continued to smile at him while he stood stunned.

"Um. Great. Do you know where it is, or would you like me to drive?"

Lena grabbed at her locket.. "Uh, no, I can drive, in case, well, in case I need to get back...before you do."

"That's fine. You know where Sunnybank is?"

"On Terhune, right? I pass it when I go to the CVS."

"Right. Terhune. Great. I'll see you there. One?" He continued jiggling his keys.

"One." She grinned.

Rick turned to go back to his office. *She said yes.* Now he had to go buy a picnic lunch somewhere. And a basket? Nah. Maybe a bagged lunch would suffice? No. Not for Lena. Rick locked up his office and told Betty he'd be out until after lunch. Rick headed to K-Mart to buy a picnic basket and, maybe, a red and white gingham tablecloth.

After snapping the blanket down on the lawn, Rick took one last look inside the basket. Two sandwiches, one turkey, one roast beef, not sure of which Lena would prefer. A can of Coke, a can of Diet Coke, two waters and two black and white cookies. He hankered for a cigarette, but he didn't want to have smoker's breath. Nor did he want to conjure up Angie, as smoking usually triggered, because he needed to have his attention, and his heart, solely on Lena. Today was about *her*. Not about his past.

Lena stood at the top of the hill overlooking Sunnybank when Rick caught a glimpse of her. He found it difficult to stand on his own two feet. He hadn't remembered ever feeling so weak in the knees. He wanted to run. Race by her side and walk her down the hill, hand in hand. But all he could do was stare. *She said yes, she'd have lunch with him at Sunnybank, and here she was.* His stomach burned with excitement.

He needed to slow the rapid breathing that took over as he watched her. Approaching him like an angel drifting in the wind, Lena showed him her wide, bright smile. He never wanted to let go this vision that now stood before him.

"Hi," she sang.

"Hi."

They stood in silence for a moment. Rick, captivated by her presence, was unable to form a coherent thought.

"It looks nice." Lena motioned to the picnic, her voice strained with nervous anticipation.

He collected himself and came back to reality. "Oh. The picnic? Yeah, well, I'm a dork." He sighed, able to bring his breathing back to normal.

She let out a gentle laugh and seemed to relax as well.

"Sit down," he requested, taking her hand as they sat down on the tablecloth. "I have turkey or roast beef." He held one up in each of his hands.

"Turkey, please," she answered, taking the sandwich.

He placed the drinks on the blanket. He took a water, she, the Diet Coke.

"I'm glad you came today," Rick started. "To be honest, I'm surprised."

Lena shrugged and responded quietly. "I'm surprised I agreed."

"Did you not want to?"

"Oh, I very much wanted to…but…I wasn't sure that I should," she said, twisting her mouth and fiddling with her fingers.

"I only intend to be a friend, Lena. Please, don't worry about that. Vince has no need to worry." Rick attempted a straight face as he said her fiancé's name.

"Oh."

Looking down at her lap, disappointment washed across her face. "Lena. What's the matter?"

"What? Nothing, why?"

"I know I've only known you just a short time," he lied, "but I feel I can read you fairly well. Something's wrong."

She shook her head. "No. Really. Nothing's wrong. It's better, actually," she offered willingly.

Rick waited, like a schoolboy expecting his first kiss, for her to continue.

"Vince and I broke up."

This *was* good news. Though he didn't want to show too much enthusiasm and risk coming across as insensitive. "Oh," he said, attempting to keep his mouth from curling up into a smile.

But then she shut down.

"Lena? Are you all right?"

"Yes."

"Did he break it off with you?"

"No." Her eyes began to swell. "I broke up with him."

"Do you regret it?"

Her tears found their way out and streamed down her cheeks. "No."

This time, though, Rick waited, aware that she wanted to say something, in her own time. So he sat and waited, then wiped her cheek with a napkin.

After a thoughtful couple of minutes, her tears slowed and she spoke.

"I shouldn't have let it get this far." Her head shook in regret. "It should have been over so, so long ago." She brought her knees up to her chest and hugged them. "He was terrible, Rick. You don't know. And I couldn't tell anyone. I wanted to, but...I thought he'd get better. And then..." She closed her eyes, recalling a bad memory, maybe? To gather courage? "Then...it was too late." Her eyes were still closed and she began to tremble.

Rick inched closer, but with Lena's eyes still closed and her arms still wrapped tight around her knees, she held up a hand. A gesture to inform him to please stay where he was, he thought. "I never wanted to...I wasn't ready...he didn't care." She swallowed hard. "He didn't even believe I was still a virgin."

Oh hell. "Lena, did he rape you?" Rick fumed, unable this time to calm his pounding heart. He wanted to throw up.

Lena's eyes flew open, once again filling with tears. But she kept them wide, like she was trying hard to keep the tears from escaping again.

"Oh, Lena." Rick's spirit deflated. "Couldn't you report him? Tell your parents? Something?"

She bit her bottom lip and leaned her head on her own shoulder, still hugging her knees, still attempting to comfort herself.

The hell with staying where he was. Lena needed to be held. He moved in closer alongside her and took her in his arms, freeing her tears.

"Lena?" Rick whispered. "Does he always force himself on you?"

Rick felt the nod on his shoulder.

"Still?"

Another nod.

"Oh, honey. I am so sorry I didn't find you sooner." Rick had his eyes closed now.

Lena lifted her head. "Found me sooner?"

"Uh, yes, I wish I had met you before he did."

She put her head back down on him. "Oh, yeah. Me too."

"Lena," Rick said almost tentatively. "That night I came over, is that what had happened? Vince, I mean?"

He felt another nod on his shoulder. This time, though, it was accompanied by a small whimper.

"Oh, sweetie. Why haven't you reported him?"

She raised her head and twisted to look at him, her tears threatening to escape again. Lena seemed determined to remain in control. "Who would believe me, Rick? I mean besides my family." Her voice got stronger as she continued. "Besides, if my father and brothers knew, they'd kill him. Then we'd have a murder on our hands. That would be worse."

Rick nodded. "It seems that'd be what he deserved though." He tried his best not to let the smoldering rage inside him explode. Lena needed him more than he needed to punch the living daylights out of Vince..

"No. No, he doesn't. Nobody deserves that."

"How could you say that, Lena? He's a monster." Rick could barely contain his anger any longer. "And he *raped* you." That word alone, used in conjunction with Lena, made him nauseous.

But with a compassionate sigh, she whispered, "He's sick, Rick. I truly believe he may be bi-polar."

Rick harrumphed. "That may be, but you can't tell me that just because he may be mentally ill, that it is okay for him to rape you and god-dammit, Lena, that is exactly what he did." Rick lost it. "Just because he is your fiancé...*was* your fiancé, doesn't mean he can *have* you any time he damn well pleases," he cried. "He is wretched…and I could kill him. I really could…"

"Hold on there, Rick," Lena interrupted, withdrawing herself from Rick's side. Standing, she continued. "Listen," she shook her head, "no, he should not have done what he had, but he wasn't *all* bad. He really had a soft side. I may be tolerant of a lot and I may put up with things he shouldn't do, but it wasn't 'cause I was so weak I couldn't pull away. It was…I guess, I felt sorry for him." She turned her back to Rick, but didn't walk away, thank God. Rick stood but didn't move closer. "He didn't know any better, Rick. He had the richest parents in town, but they'd barely paid any attention to him. He grew up with one nanny after another, no one ever really showing him any love…he couldn't help how he was."

"Lena." Rick proceeded cautiously, knowing he was on thin ice. "Everybody has a past to get over. There is *never* an excuse to hurt another human being." Rick realized the irony of his statement after recalling previously wanting to kill Vince.

Lena shuddered, slumping her shoulders forward. "No. I know you're right…I just don't want to believe he could be deliberately malicious."

Rick went ahead and moved toward her, placing his hand on her shoulder as she stood still looking toward the lake.

"At least it's over, Lena. At least it's over."

Chapter Fifteen

Lena felt bad defending Vince, but they had encountered some good moments in their relationship and she did feel sympathetic toward him. At times, she really thought Vince could never evolve into a mature human being. All the drugs he had done, and the lack of nurturing, surely contributed to his immaturity. Violence was never okay, but Lena knew that Vince had some kind of chemical imbalance, and if he had ever admitted to needing help, she was certain he could get well.

But Rick had been right. It was no excuse. She could no longer be the brunt of Vince's shortcomings. Though her heart sank for Vince, she had to admit, she was glad it was over.

Lena turned toward Rick. "Yeah, it's over." She sighed. There was an awkward silence before Lena noticed Rick gazing at her mouth, then her eyes, then her mouth again. Lena had involuntarily done the same to Rick, but as he leaned forward, she bent her neck so that his mouth brushed the top of her head. She closed her eyes, afraid of Rick's reaction. She bit her upper lip and cringed. How horrible she must have made him feel, but she could not allow him to kiss her. She'd only just broken up with Vince. It was unjustifiable. As much as the thought of Rick's beautiful mouth on hers drove her wild, she felt an obligation to mourn the death of her engagement, for at least a little while.

Rick just shrugged it off. He put his arm around Lena and led them back to the tablecloth. "C'mon. Let's eat. We'll probably need to head back to the office soon."

They sat. He took a bite of his sandwich, but she just sipped her soda. After all the emotions she'd just experienced, her stomach felt queasy and she had no desire to eat. Rick seemed to notice. "Lena, if you'd rather have something sweet." He rummaged through the basket and pulled out a white bag. "I have a couple black and white cookies." He handed her the white bag.

"Black and white cookies?" She looked in the bag and pulled one out. "Oh my goodness, I love these things." Her stomach may have felt funny, but for a black and white, she'd deal with it. "You know, these were my great-great-grandmother's favorites. Of course, I never knew her, but Mimi tells me every time she brings them over."

"Mimi?"

"Oh, that's my great-gram. My mom's grandmother."

"Wow. She's still alive?"

Lena chuckled. "Of course, she's only ninety."

Now Rick laughed. "*Only* ninety? I say that's quite an accomplishment."

"Yeah, well, Mimi's great. Her mom had her young. She was only fifteen. I don't know, Mimi tells me her mom married an older man, and he insisted they marry young or something. She never finished school or anything."

"Who? Your Mimi?"

"Oh no, my Mimi's mother."

"Ah." Rick's eyes glazed over, as if he were recalling something important.

"Anyway, my great-grandmother thinks I've inherited her mother's love for black and white cookies." Lena giggled again.

"Cute." Rick still kept his gaze on Lena, and although she could sit and look at his perfectly assembled face all day, it was making her uncomfortable. Not in the creepy sort of way but in the *'Oh my God, I could just jump him'* sort of way. And that was an unsettling emotion for Lena, because never ever did she ever want to jump anyone.

She nibbled at her black and white cookie, savoring each little bite. As she broke off a piece of her cookie, she looked up at Rick, who was watching her. "What?" she asked, smiling.

He smiled back at her. "Why don't you come with me Friday night to The Tavern? I can pick you up, we can eat, then I'll do my gig and we can...get a cup of coffee somewhere."

She thought about it.

"Can I take you out?" He waited patiently for an answer, while she contemplated the question.

"Why not," she answered, not meaning to sound so indifferent. She wanted nothing more than to go on a date with Rick, she just had to convince herself that it was okay.

Rick's ego had been punctured. He'd hoped for a more enthusiastic response. "If I'm troubling you my dear, you *are* allowed to say no," he retorted, although he'd been trying for a more lighthearted response.

"Rick. I really would like to go with you. I hadn't meant to sound so...flippant. I just couldn't help worrying about what Vince would do. But...it really isn't his business anymore. I need to break totally free from him."

"It's okay, Lena. Really."

Lena felt her face flush. She had a date with Rick Murphy. She couldn't wait.

Chapter Sixteen

He came to the door with a bouquet of flowers already in a vase. His auburn hair, slicked back with a little gel, instead of his usual tousled hair, was darn sexy. So were his charcoal button-down shirt and black flat-front Dockers. His black motorcycle boots completed his dark ensemble. Rick Murphy looked bad in black, and Lena was definitely hot for him. But she couldn't let him know that. Not yet.

"Good evening, Lena," Rick breathed, after an exaggerated pause.

"Hi." Lena sighed, more dreamily than she'd meant to.

"You look lovely tonight."

Lena looked down at her light-gray mini-skirt, lavender blouse, black tights and Mary-Janes. "Oh…thanks," she said, feeling her skin grow warm.

"These are for you." The assortment of lilies of the valley, with one pink rose in the center, was daintily set in a slender iridescent vase with a pale pink satin ribbon tied around it.

"Oh, Rick, they're so pretty. They're perfect. Thank you so much."

Lena watched his face light up with pride. "You're welcome. Why don't you put them down and we can get going…if you're ready, I mean."

"I am." She put the vase on her coffee table and slipped on her purple cardigan before grabbing her small black purse and locking the door.

"Thank you for joining me tonight," Lena heard Rick say from behind her, as they headed down the stairs. "I'm really looking forward to it."

"Me too." Lena had been looking forward to going out with Rick and watching him perform, but eating in front of him made her nervous. Her stomach felt queasy at the idea. Nibbling on a black and white cookie and barely eating her pasta at their "business" lunch were one thing, but eating a whole meal? Would she not be aware of food left on her mouth or in-between her teeth? Certain she'd make a fool of herself one way or the other, she tried to force the thought out of her head. Acting all jittery in front of him wouldn't earn her any points in composure.

Rick seemed to know everyone at The Tavern, since every patron excitedly called him by name as he walked into the pub. He'd high-five them as they passed. It reminded Lena of old

Cheers episodes, where they all yelled 'Norm' as the large man walked into the bar. Seeing Rick so popular with the crowd added to Lena's jitters. She may have been born into a huge family, but large crowds still made her anxious. Add to that the attention Rick was receiving, her uneasiness was amplified.

As if he sensed her anxiety, Rick took her by the hand and pulled her close. He led them to a semi-private table in the corner near the stage and pulled out her chair to sit.

"Thank you," Lena replied to his gallantry.

A waitress came to the table just as Rick sat down in his chair across from her. "Hey Ricky, the usual?" She grinned ear to ear at Ricky while she waited for his reply.

"Not tonight, Gina." Rick turned to Lena. "What would you like, Lena?"

"Oh, just a diet coke, please."

"And I'll have a Corona, please," Rick answered, then turned his attention to Lena before the waitress left the table.

"So," Lena asked Rick. "What's your usual?"

"A Whisky Sour."

"Isn't that an old man's drink?"

Rick laughed, then shrugged. "I'm an old man."

"No you're not," Lena said, before realizing she hadn't known how old Rick actually was. "How are old are you?"

"Thirty-seven."

Lena eyebrows shot up.

"See. Old."

Lena smiled. "No, that's not old, just…"

"Older than you," he finished.

"You don't look thirty-seven."

"Ah. No backpedaling." He laughed.

Lena chuckled. "I'm not. But really, I thought you were like twenty-eight or something like that."

"Mmm. Something like that."

The mischievous way he shot his eyes up and smirked had Lena tingling in places she was unaware were able to tingle. The sexiness he embodied, stirred in her an arousal so volcanic, she hoped she wouldn't explode right there. She couldn't understand her body's uncontrollable attraction to the man sitting in front of her. Certainly she'd been in the presence of good-looking men before. What made this one so different?

"So Lena, what are your weekends like?" Rick decided, she guessed, to change gears and talk about something other than his age.

"Well." She needed to think about this, considering this was her first full weekend alone without the burden of Vince's plans on her agenda. "Usually I do whatever Vince has planned, but now that he's…out of the picture, I'm kind of looking forward to reading some books I've put aside."

"Ah. Quiet time."

"Mmm," Lena thought. "What do you do on the weekends?"

Rick took a moment to gather his thoughts. "Well, I do a lot of work on my land, tend to my horses, go see my broth…I hang out. You know, take it easy."

"Take it easy? Tending to your land and horses sounds like just the opposite of taking it easy. What do you do on your land? Farm?"

Rick guffawed. Really loud.

"What's so funny?"

"I don't know the first thing about farming. I'm a city boy at heart. I bought the land because it had a wonderful barn to renovate."

Lena looked at him silently, hopefully encouraging him to continue. He was such an interesting fellow. Simple, yet complicated.

"I'm turning my barn into a huge rec room. A place to hang out, write music, record. Stuff like that."

"You *write* music?" An impressed Lena asked.

"I do. I enjoy it."

"And you record your stuff?"

"Only to send out as demos. I write songs for other's to play. In fact, one of the bands I wrote for many years ago…their drummer's here to perform with me tonight."

"Oh? Who?" Rick was amazingly versatile, thought Lena.

"Matty Em from the group Holland. Are you too young to remember them?"

"No. I've heard of them. I'm not *that* young. Besides, my cousin Mara is dating the lead singer."

"What? Tagg Holland?" asked Rick, eyebrows shooting towards his hairline.

"Yeah, she started dating him last year; he's opening up a music camp for the underprivileged soon."

"Wow, yeah, I'd heard that, Camp Holland, right?"

"Yeah."

"Anyway, Matty's in the area this weekend, probably visiting Tagg, so I asked him to play with me tonight. It's sort of a surprise for the bar. So, shhh." Rick put his finger to his smiling lips.

"Did you ever think of..." Lena paused to say this just right, so not to offend Rick in any way. "I don't know...keeping your songs for yourself and..." She couldn't seem to find the right words without sounding shallow.

"Trying to make it in the music business?"

Lena simply nodded.

"No. Not for me. I like my quiet life. I like the crowd I perform for. I like riding my horses and my motorcycle. I like my life. It's...almost perfect."

"Almost?"

"I'm only missing one thing." Lena could hear forlorn in his voice. After waiting for Rick to proceed with his statement, she realized he wasn't intending to fill her in on what was missing in his life.

So she decided it was her turn to change the subject. She caught something in what he'd said before and wondered about it. "Rick, before, you mentioned that you go see your brother on the weekends, but I thought you had said once that you were an only child?"

His eyes grew wide, as if he were caught with his hand in the cookie jar.

"Oh. Um. You caught that huh?" Rick asked. "I meant my grandmother's brother. My great-uncle. He's ninety-nine this year. I visit him every now and then, since she's not around anymore…So, um, let me go see what's taking Gina so long with our food."

And he was up and gone from the table in an instant. Lena wondered what that was about. What about his uncle left Rick so tight-lipped? Well, it's not that big of a deal. Lena was having a nice time with Rick. She wasn't going to let a little secret, especially one so inconsequential, ruin her night.

Now if she could only get rid of her stomachache. Those butterflies were wreaking havoc tonight.

Lena and Rick were just about done with dinner when Lindsey, Betty and Gary showed up. "Hey, you two." Lindsey beamed.

"Hey," Lena and Rick said in unison.

"Hey, guys," Rick greeted Betty and Gary, who lagged behind Lindsey a bit.

"Hey, Rick, I see you got a drum set up there tonight. You playing?" Lindsey asked.

"Nope." Rick was wearing a huge grin.

"Who is?'

"A friend of mine," was all he'd say. "Listen guys, you mind keeping Lena company? I see my *friend* is here and I'd like to talk to him." Rick winked at Lena.

Up on the make-shift stage, Rick sat on a stool, his guitar strapped around him, his hand on the microphone. "Hey y'all."

The Tavern patrons hooted and hollered.

"Who out there remembers the band, Holland?"

More hootin'. More hollerin'.

"Well, then I guess y'all remember a little drummer named Matty Em?"

Now the crowd went wild. They stood. They clapped. They relished in the company of famed drummer, Matty Em, from the 90s band, Holland.

Matty ran out on stage, waving and thanking the audience for the generous welcome. He took his seat behind the drums and began tapping the rims with his sticks.

Rick, still seated upon his stool, stomped his foot along with Matty's beat. Clapping his hands above his head, directing the crowd to do the same, Rick began singing. "Yeah, yeah, yeah, yeah," and invited everyone to do the same. After a couple of lines of 'yeah, yeah…,' Rick sang the first two verses of the song with only the beat of Matty's drum, the crowd clapping to the beat, and Rick's heel meeting the floor at the same intervals.

Lena recognized the song. It was a popular song she heard on the radio all the time.

He was good, she thought. Rick's voice was nice. Smooth. Rick exuded confidence up there. Lena got pretty turned on watching him entertain the crowd. Every now and then he'd turn his head in her direction and wink. Those warm feelings she had earlier were returning.

When they finished the song, Rick walked over to Matty to say something, then she heard the drum. Rick started on his guitar. Lena didn't recognize the song, but the crowd seemed to know it. She liked the upbeat tune, yet the words conveyed a relationship that could never be. Something about the girl being part of a past that the boy could no longer return to. It was really good. She'd wondered why she hadn't heard it before. Lena made a mental note to ask Rick about it later.

After about an hour, Rick and Matty informed everyone they were taking a break. Rick pulled up a seat next to Lena. She handed him a cold beer that Gina had placed on the table about two minutes before the break. Gina seemed to know his routine pretty well…and she didn't appear to like Lena very much.

"So, did you enjoy it?" Rick asked Lena after he took a sip of his beer.

"I did. Very much so." Lena beamed at the handsomely sweaty man in front of her. "You're an awesome musician."

"Thanks." He wiped his brow with his sleeve and took another swig of beer.

"When did you learn to play?"

"I'm not really sure. It was just something I've always been able to do."

Impressed, Lena asked, "Really? Do you play any other instruments besides guitar?"

Lindsey laughed. "Are you kidding me, Lena? This man's a one-man band. He can play anything."

Lena turned to Rick, who was now red with embarrassment. "Lena, honey, I'll be right back. I just have to see a man about a horse." Then he kissed her on the forehead and left.

That was an odd expression, Lena thought. She could remember her great-grandfather using that phrase frequently, when he was still alive.

"So isn't he awesome, Lena? God, you are so lucky," Lindsey whispered, when Rick was out of earshot.

"Lucky? Why?"

"Why? Because Rick adores you. Even Gary said so. He told me Rick was so happy you weren't with Vince anymore."

"Oh." Lena blushed but didn't really know what to say.

"And, oh, it is killing Gina that you are with him tonight. She's had her eye on him for years. He went out with her once or twice, but she said he had been stuck on some girl from his past, but she still keeps trying."

"Is he still stuck on that girl?"

"Gina?"

"No. The one from his past." Lena felt a flicker of jealousy, and she didn't like it. Not usually the jealous type, here she sat, upset that Rick had a past. He's thirty-seven years old. Of course he had a past.

"Oh, I don't really know. I told you he doesn't like to date and when he does, it's usually the girl who initiates it. But, here you are. And Gary told me Rick asked you, not the other way around, so, hey, maybe you're just what he needed to get over his past."

Lena pondered that for a while. She hoped there was some kind of future for her and Rick. He'd certainly reawakened her soul. And her heart was finally, genuinely smiling.

Chapter Seventeen

The Tavern had emptied out by 2am. Rick performed longer than usual since he had Matty joining him. He worried that Lena was bored or tired. He knew she'd never say so, being so polite and all, but he worried just the same. What kind of man brings a girl out on a first date…and hardly spends any time with her? He needed to make a better impression.

He paid Jack his tab and said good-night to the owner. "You ready, Lena?" He sighed, sorry the night had to end. He helped to pull out her chair as she got up, then took her hand. With her hand in his, they slowly walked to the car. There was a nip in the air tonight, so Rick took his hand from Lena's and wrapped his arm around her. "I owe you another date, I think."

"What? What d'you mean?" Lena's contorted expression signaled bewilderment.

"I mean," Rick turned her by the arm to look at him when they reached his Jeep. "I owe you a real date. One where I'm actually an active participant in *said* date." Rick grinned, emphasizing his playfulness.

"Oh." Lena laughed. "Rick, I had a wonderful time. You were awesome up there tonight."

"Yeah, up there." He pointed toward the bar. "But on a date, I shouldn't have been…up there. I should have been right here," he said, pointing at the spot in front of her. Then he held her with his finger and thumb by the chin and kissed her tenderly on the lips. "Can I take you out tomorrow night?"

"Really? You don't *have* to."

"Well, unless you'd rather read those books you've been waiting on?"

Another gentle chuckle came from Lena. "No. I'd much rather see *you* than read." Her face turned a lovely shade of pink and Rick thought, *at long last, I've found what I've been searching for.*

Later that night, sitting in his recliner, he had no desire to light a cigarette. No desire to reach the girl from his past. He was quite content…right here in the present.

****

Lena put her head on her pillow that night and smiled to herself as she closed her eyes and thought about this evening. Being with Rick felt wonderful. His hand felt just right when he held hers. His kiss was …perfect on her lips. When he hugged her goodbye at her door, she knew that in his arms she was meant to be…like being lost…and finding her way back home. Words really couldn't describe the comfort and safety she felt when Rick held her, but the feelings were there. Whether she could describe them or not, Rick was where she needed to be…who she'd been *destined* to be with.

That was the last thought that blanketed her mind before she fell asleep…the last thought before her nightly dreams took over. Only this time, they didn't start off horribly.

He had his guitar across his lap, tapping on it like it was a drum. She peered out her door.

"What are you doing here? I saw you from the window." She held herself in nervous composure. If Mother wakes…and…and …finds me…out here with you…well, she will just have my hide…and yours."

"Angie." He smiled up at her, melting her heart. "You are…so…lovely." He stood to greet her.

"Oh, Richard, stop. I mean it. If Mother sees you, I will be in so much trouble."

"Do you have a book on you?"

"Yes. You know I always do." Angie reached inside her apron pocket and pulled out her favorite book, Elizabeth Bennet or, Pride and

Prejudice. *"But what does that have to do with your being here?"*

"Well." Richard's *demonic grin implied something was up his sleeve. "If your sorry excuse for a mother wakes up from her drunken coma,* I *will run back to the store and* you *can say you were out here reading."*

"Richar..."

"Shh." He put his fingers to Angie's mouth. "Sit. I *want to play you something."*

They sat down on her front stoop.

"I have been working on this," he said, as *he played his guitar. "I do not have the words yet, but I have been working on the melody. If you are ever allowed to come to my house, I can play it on our piano for you, but until then, my guitar will have to do."*

Angie sighed.

"Just listen."

His fingers on the guitar moved as if they were part of the instrument – the sound coming from it, soft and pleasant. He hummed while he played. Angie closed her eyes and rocked side to side to the slow melody of his guitar playing.

Lena roused, the mellow musical tune still in her head, the feeling of love, still in her heart. She thought of Richard...and his fingers on the guitar...the passion she felt for the teenage boy who sat beside her. The teenage boy? Richard?

Lena opened her eyes. My goodness. It was only a dream. A darn dream. A blessed dream. At least this dream had been a happy one. It reminded her of her date last night with Rick. And they had another date waiting on the horizon. She couldn't wait for tonight, to see Rick again. Lena hadn't felt this exuberant in a long time. She no longer had the feeling of a heavy heart weighing her down. No longer did she have to be afraid of Vince, he was out of her life.

It was only eight in the morning, and Lena had nothing to do until later this evening. But she was too wound up to get back to sleep. Instead, she got herself a cup of coffee and brought it to her room. Reading a book while propped up in bed under the warm covers was one of her favorite things to do. She had been wanting to re-read her Jane Austen novels, and today would be perfect for reading a classic.

The time went by quite quickly when Lena had a novel in hand. Had the buzzing of her cell phone not brought her back to reality, she wouldn't have been aware that it was already eleven o'clock.

"Hello?" She managed to get to her phone, before it turned over to voicemail.

"Good Morning, Lena." She heard the familiar warm voice on the other end. "Did I allow you to sleep-in long enough?"

"Hi, Rick. I've been up a while now." Lena couldn't believe he called her so early. That must mean that he enjoyed last night as much as she did.

Even though, like he said, they didn't spend all that much time together.

"I was wondering if, instead of waiting until this evening, I could pick you up this afternoon. I'd like to spend the day with you…If you don't mind?"

She'd love to! "Oh, sure, that'd be nice. When? I'm not ready right now."

"How 'bout in an hour? I'll take you to lunch."

Oh my goodness, an hour? To get ready? Really? "An hour's perfect," Lena lied.

"Good. I'll pick you up at noon."

Lena could not believe it. He wanted to spend the day with her. What would she wear? She couldn't get too dressed up. Who knows what they would be doing the rest of the day. Should she wear a miniskirt, jeans, leggings? And oh my goodness, what shoes?

Well those dilemmas would have to wait until after her shower. She needed time to let her hair air-dry a little before she blew it dry.

Promptly, Rick rang her doorbell…at precisely twelve noon. She checked herself in the mirror. Gap jeans, brown Durango boots, white tee, sienna-colored hoodie with a leather pull-string. Her dark brownish-black hair was pulled into two loose side ponytails. She'd contemplated that decision one more quick time, but decided she liked her hair in two ponytails and so what if she looked like a teenager. She liked her style.

The doorbell rang again. "Oh my goodness," Lena cried out loud. She'd forgotten he was at the door. She grabbed her purse off the bed, ran down the stairs, and opened the door. "Hey Rick," she huffed, out of breath from running down the stairs. Boy, she thought, she'd better start exercising if running down two flights of stairs had her gasping for air. "Sorry about that."

"No problem. If you need more time, I don't mind waiting."

"No. I'm good," she claimed, as she reached behind her to pull the door shut.

"You look sweet, Lena." Rick took her hand and headed toward his Jeep. "I thought we'd take a ride up to Sugar Loaf to have lunch. Have you ever been?"

"Sugar Loaf? No. Is that a restaurant?"

Rick chuckled. "It's a town. In New York State."

Lena smiled.

"It's an artsy type of community. Lots of crafty stuff. Just under the Sugar Loaf Mountain up route 23...near Warwick."

"Oh, I've never heard of it."

"I think you'll like it," he said, as he started the car.

With the roof and doors off the jeep, Lena's decision to put her hair in two ponytails had been a good idea. The warm breeze mimicked sixty mile per hour winds as they drove the highway northbound. The sensation thrilled her, as did the presence of the man in the driver's seat.

The Barnsider Tavern was a cozy two-story pub and restaurant, quaint, with a fireplace on both floors.

"So, where'd you find out about this place?" Lena wondered.

"A few years ago, a band I used to play with had a gig here. I like it up here." The waiter came with their drink order. Rick raised his beer mug to Lena. "To us."

Lena smiled, clinking her diet coke to his mug. "To us." Lena blushed. "So... do you come to Sugar Loaf a lot?"

Rick shrugged. "Not often, no. I met this woman up here once..."

"Oh," Lena exhaled.

Rick grinned, apparently appreciating the flattery. "No, Lena, not like that. This woman was," he took a breath, "a psychic of sorts."

"A psychic?" Lena marveled. "You believe in psychics?"

"To a point, I guess...I don't know...she helped me get through some ...stuff...I suppose."

"Did she tell you about your future?"

Rick chuckled. "No. Not about my future...more about my past."

"Oh." The girl from the song, Lena remembered.

"What...Oh?" Rick asked of her quick comment.

"Just…oh." Rick peered at Lena and she resumed, "Lindsey told me you had a hard time getting over a girl."

"She did, did she? Well, Lindsey thinks she knows everything, I think."

"You *didn't* have a hard time getting over a girl?"

Rick focused his eyes on Lena's. His gaze was intense…sending little trickles of excitement through her. "Yes…I did, but…it's complicated and…" Rick became pensive momentarily, then shrugged. "I'm done getting over her."

Lena glowed from the inside out. "Good."

"Yes. It's very good."

****

After lunch, Rick showed Lena *Romer's Alley*, a street in Sugar Loaf that was a village in itself. He took joy in their hand-in-hand walk through the gardens and watching her peruse the *Moondancer* and other specialty shops. He loved finally having this time with her. He never wanted to let her go.

"I'm having a really nice time today, Rick. Thank you for taking me here."

Rick looked down at Lena and squeezed her hand. The warmth of the afternoon sunlight, and the way it glistened off of Lena's brown eyes, punctuated the perfectness of the day.

"You're very welcome. I'm having a really nice time, as well."

They walked quietly for a while, before turning back and heading home.

In Rick's jeep, he turned on the radio and let the classic rock station fill the car with a Fleetwood Mac song. He knew the song well, because his mom listened to Stevie Nicks frequently during his childhood. A 70s hit was the song playing on the radio, and while he listened, his heart overflowed with happiness. The song was *Dreams,* and for years he had only to dream of the love he'd longed for. Now, as if by magic, she appeared true-to-life, no longer a figment of his imagination. No longer an illusion from his past.

Rick's only regret was that Lena had no memory of that past. He'd do what he could to jog that memory, but if he couldn't, then he'd just have to work hard at getting her to fall in love with him…all over again.

Chapter Eighteen

That night, Lena felt wonderful. No longer burdened with Vince's anger and elated with Rick's affection, as soon as her head hit the pillow, she fell asleep. Never one fortunate enough to fall into a dreamless slumber, sometime during the night, Lena's imagination turned on full-throttle.

"Mom," twenty-five year-old Emmie began. "Why have you been so down lately? Can I help?"

"Oh Emmie, you do help, always. I've just been thinking about our life. Since your brothers and sisters have moved out of the house, I was wondering if we should take a trip somewhere."

"How can we though? I am in a wheelchair, you do not drive...and we have no money."

"Emmie, it is all right. I have enough saved up for a bus trip. I have always wanted to see the ocean. Are you up for it?"

"I am, Mom. That sounds wonderful."

They took the bus down Route Nine until it reached Seaside Heights, New Jersey. Angelina pushed Emmie up the ramp onto the most exciting site she had ever seen. The long vertical strips of wood were nailed together to form the longest walkway Angelina had ever seen. And it formed the perfect platform for the beauty of God's artwork. Angelina and Emmie stood along the two metal parallel bars that came between them and the blue-black body of water that rumbled before them.

Angelina had longed to see the ocean water since she was thirteen years old. It was a bittersweet emotion. She was so happy to be experiencing the view with her youngest, most special child, Emmie, but her thoughts were of Richard and how different her life might have turned out had he not gone off to war. Automatically, Angelina's hand went to her necklace. The gift from Richard that was now only half a locket. Angelina's thoughts went back to the day she handed Richard the other half of her locket. The day he left for the war.

And never returned.

Had Richard survived, she would have run off with him after witnessing a murder on the way home from school, instead of into the arms of Timothy. A man, twice her age, who had promised to protect her. A man, who at thirty years old, thought it appropriate to rape a fifteen year-

old...and get her pregnant.   Then beat her, relentlessly.

Had Richard survived, they would have followed their plans to marry, and her life would have been filled with joy...not sorrow. But he had not survived. And she married that vile man, who, after impregnating her seven times, had an affair and bore a love child during their marriage.

Richard had not survived...and Angelina had...much to her chagrin.

Lena awoke overwhelmed with sadness once again. Her dream, which began on a sweet note, turned heavy with woe. The true-to-life emotions in her night's vision had hit her hard. Who was Angelina? Could it *be* her great-great-grandmother? A chill ran up Lena's spine. She had an eerie feeling about it, but couldn't put her finger on it.

Mimi had spoken of her mother's life, but never in detail. Hopefully, Lena's imagination was just fabricating a story based on Mimi's tales.

But the locket. It was the one Lena wore *every day*. The locket she had been drawn to inexplicably since she found it in Mimi's jewelry box as a child. Mimi never knew the story behind it.   She only knew her mother wore it every day...without explanation...until the day she'd died.

And who was Richard? She had dreamed of a Richard before. The photo in the locket too faded to recognize, could it be the same man? Could Nana have had a lover who went off to war and never returned?

Still, why would Lena be dreaming about Nana's life? And what did it have to do with Lena?

****

Rick woke up on cloud nine. He had the best day of his life yesterday and couldn't wait for more. Being so physically close to Lena, aroused an intensity in Rick's emotions he hadn't felt in a long-time. Maybe not *ever* in his thirty-seven years. With her, he was home. His love for Lena Giordano ran deep, and he hoped one day she'd feel it too.

He readied himself for his weekly visit to see Andrew. Rick made it a point to see him every week without fail, because at ninety-nine years old, Andrew's days were numbered. Andrew was important to Rick. So important that he hated to think just how little time he had left. Rick owed Andrew so much. When he had felt alienated and scared, Andrew had comforted him. When Rick fell apart, Andrew picked up the pieces and made Rick almost whole again. That was nearly twenty years ago.

Lakeview Care Center was always busiest on Sunday afternoons. Rick routinely contemplated visiting Andrew some other day of the week, but Sundays just always seemed most appropriate. There were fewer activities scheduled for the residents, since most were busy with their visiting relatives, and Rick was usually tied up with work during the week.

Andrew's eyes were closed when Rick walked in. All too aware of Andrew's fragility, Rick approached him slowly and quietly, grazing his forearm tenderly to let him know he was there. Though his eyelashes fluttered meagerly, Rick knew Andrew was cognizant of his presence.

"Hey, Andy."

Andrew's eyes darted beneath their lids.

"Hey buddy, I went on a date with Angie. Remember I told you about her? She's Lena now." Rick paused, waiting for any movement at all from Andrew. "She doesn't remember me, but…that's ok…as long as I can get her to fall in love with me again." A tear fell from Rick's eye. It landed on Andrew's hand. "Sorry about that, buddy." Rick wiped it off. "Andrew, I owe you…you helped me, guy. Because of you, I don't think I'm crazy anymore. Well…maybe a little…but not like pschitzo or anything."

Rick closed his eyes and rested his forehead on Andrew's arm. He welcomed the memory of August 16, 1992:

Seventeen-year-old Rick was sick to his stomach, the acids churning, making him want to puke. The images in his head were overwhelming. No longer could Rick decipher reality from make-

believe. The doctors wanted to put him in the psych ward at Chilton Memorial, and his mother agreed. That was two weeks earlier. Since then, Rick had been hiding out at one friend or another's, pleading for their confidentiality.

He approached the building on Grand Street in Paterson. It was still a storefront but no longer a market. A television repair shop now stood in its place...the upstairs apartment now painted blue, instead of white. The windows and doors had also been replaced. But it was definitely John's Mercantile – his father's store – the store he left at age seventeen years-old, the exact age he was now, yet seventy-five years ago.

Rick felt uneasy. Probably no one inside had ever even heard of him, yet the call to be here was undeniable. A bell rang when Rick opened the glass door.

"Can I help you, young man?" A heavy-set man in denim asked.

"Um, sure." Rick trembled. "I...uh...was wondering if you've ever heard of a man named Andrew Grossi? He used to live here a long time ago."

"Sure. Andy. He's still here. Lives upstairs. Friendly old man."

Rick's stomach swirled anxiously about. Had his visions been correct? Andrew Grossi really existed? "He...he...still lives here?"

"Still owns the place. He's my landlord."

"Really?" Rick felt his heart swell as a lump formed in his throat. He wanted to cry.

"How do you know him?"

How did *he* know *him?* *"Actually, I...uh...don't. My...*grandmother *told me stories about him. She's not here anymore, but...I always think about him."*

"Ah. Let me give him a call. Maybe he'll come down." The man picked up a phone behind the counter. *"What was your grandmother's name, son?"*

"Oh...I don't want you to call him down. He must be so old..."

"Nonsense. He may be seventy-nine, but he's sprite as a sixty year-old I tell you." He motioned that the phone was ringing. *"Her name?"* he whispered, while covering the mouthpiece of the receiver.

"Angelina...Angelina Maria Mancini." Rick hoped Andrew would have known her. He would have been only four years-old when Richard died, but he was sure Andrew had grown up to know Angie.

The television man hung up the phone. *"Andy said he thinks he knows who you are talking about. He'll be right down."*

Rick nodded and fumbled with the change in his pocket.

"So, you from around here?" the man asked.

"No. Pompton Lakes."

"Aah, nice area."

"Mmm hmm," Rick responded, too nervous to hold a conversation with the rotund man behind the counter.   Meeting Andrew Grossi would confirm whether Rick's memories were real or fabricated. Whether Rick was stable-minded...or on the brink of mental illness.

The moment of truth had arrived.   In from the back door walked a small old man dressed in dark shorts and a white golf shirt.

"Andy," the T.V. man announced. "How are ya, guy?"

"I'm good, guy, you?

"Can't complain."

The lean silver-haired older man turned his attention toward Rick. "So, Son, how do you know Angelina Mancini? You're kinda young there, aren't you? I heard she passed years ago. Was she your great-grandmother or something?"

"Uh, no, Sir." Rick took a nervous swallow, "She was..." Rick didn't even know how to begin. "It's a long story.   Is there somewhere we can talk?"

The nurse interrupted Rick's trip back in time.   "Sorry, Mr. Murphy, I need to check his vitals. I'll only be a minute. You can stay."

"No, I think I should be going." Rick stood from his seat. "Has he been sleeping a lot?" he asked the nurse.

Her facial expression solemn, she answered, "Yes…it will not be long, sweetheart. I'm sorry."

Rick left the nursing home deflated. For the past twenty years, Andrew had been a mainstay in Rick's life. Now it was coming to an end. He hated to bear it. Andrew would be missed. But it was probably time he moved on.

Chapter Nineteen

Lena parked her electric-green Ford Focus under the maple tree that sat in the right corner of Mimi's front yard. Mimi's red-brick Dutch Colonial was always a haven for Lena – a place to enjoy all the sugary treats Lena's own mom would never allow growing up. Mimi would let Lena indulge in a jar full of marshmallow Fluff or even a Fluffer-Nutter sandwich for lunch. Though Mimi now lived with her younger sister Rose, twenty-five year old Lena still felt like an adolescent schoolgirl sneaking treats behind her mother's back when she visited Mimi's home.

True to a usual visit with Mimi, there were yummy cakes in the glass-covered pedestal cake plate and cookies in the old Mickey Mouse cookie jar. Mimi put on a kettle of water and placed two honey-vanilla tea bags in two pink rose covered tea cups. After some small talk and treat gathering,

Mimi and Lena brought their refreshments into the Florida room in the back of the house.

"So, dear, what can I help you with?" Mimi's gentle voice was a hug out loud. Lena could feel the warmth and compassion in every word Mimi spoke.

"Oh Mimi, I've been so...confused, I guess you could say." Lena slid sideways on the couch so that she was now sitting on her left foot and holding her tea on her lap. "You know that I have such a crazy imagination."

Mimi nodded, along with letting out a slight snicker in agreement.

Lena chuckled along with her. "Well, anyway...my dreams have been kind of crazy lately also. I keep having these dreams about the same girl. Angelina, like Nana's name."

Mimi smiled at the sound of her mother's name. "And like your name, dear...don't forget."

Lena blushed. "I know, Mimi. It's just...this girl wasn't me. I...actually think it *was* Nana."

Mimi nodded.

"The girl looked like pictures you have of her."

A smiling Mimi asked, "Has Nana been on your mind lately?"

Lena sat quietly, elbow against the back cushion, her head resting on her hand. She thought about her conversation with Rick – the black and white cookie conversation. "I guess so."

"Well then, it's quite natural then," Mimi reassured, "to dream about someone you're thinking of."

"I guess so," Lena repeated. "But...there was this other...person. In my dream. A boy. A guy named Richard."

Mimi jutted her chin and shook her head.

"Nana didn't know a Richard?" Lena asked.

"Not that I know of dear."

Lena grabbed hold of her locket just then, brought it to her lips, and kissed it. She had no idea why an old thin piece of gold meant so much to her, but suddenly, she needed answers. "Mimi?"

"Yes, dear?"

"Tell me about this locket?" Lena asked quietly.

Mimi laughed. "Oh, dear, I wish I could. The only thing I know about it is that your Nana, my mother, wore it every single day of her life. Broken and all."

"She never told you where she got it?"

Mimi shook her head. "No."

"Do you know why she wore it?"

"No...why? What is this? Why do you need to know about the locket all of a sudden?"

"Why did you keep it? I mean...it was in your jewelry box when I found it."

"Yes, dear," Mimi blurted. "It obviously was important to my mother. She'd had it on the day she'd died. I thought better of leaving it on her when they were to close her casket. I mean...it's not like her soul stays in there with her, right?"

"No." Lena shook her head. "No, I guess not."

"Anyway," Mimi continued. "It was a tiny thing and...it couldn't hurt any to keep it. Besides, you've really taken a liking to it."

Yeah. But why, Lena thought, why does this broken locket mean so much to her?

Monday morning, all Lena could think about was Nana, Richard...and Rick. Why Rick? What did he have to do with all of this? It didn't make sense. Maybe Lena's imagination fabricated the stories in her head. It would not be so far-fetched for Lena to do so. She was spending more and more time with Rick. They'd spoken about her Nana. She'd mentioned her locket to him, she was sure. Lena probably just melded everything together. Making up stories in that imaginative mind of hers. She chuckled to herself and put her mind on her PR work.

Anxious to see Rick once lunchtime rolled around, she practically raced to Sunnybank Park...knowing full well he'd be there waiting for her.

Chapter Twenty

Rick's heart thundered beneath his chest when Lena's Ford Focus made its way down the gravel slope. Sheer excitement took over just thinking about her. Since Saturday's drive to Sugar Loaf, aside from his concern for Andrew, Rick's mind was adrift with thoughts of Lena. Thoughts of holding her, kissing her, loving her.

When she pulled next to the Jeep, Rick opened her car door, and by hand, drew her out of the car and led her to the stone seat that overlooked Sunnybank Park and its cozy lake.

Still embracing her hand while they settled on the bench, Rick apprised Lena of the wonderful time he'd had on Saturday.

"I had a nice time as well. Thank you so much for taking me there," she said, showing a most radiant smile.

"Anytime," Rick thought, as he said it aloud, feeling his heart rate picking up speed again.

"Did you go see your uncle yesterday?" Lena's knee jostled, while her genteel face betrayed her obvious anxiety.

Rick thought to himself that she too must be smitten, as he was. This put a smile on his face. He felt it spread from ear to ear.

"Does that smile mean you went to see him?" Lena interrupted his silent rejoicing.

"Oh." Rick shook his head. "No, it does not. My smile was merely a response to your beautiful face." Oh, geez, he sounded like a fruitcake. He noticed Lena blush. "Actually, I did go to see him." His smile disappeared. "My uncle...is not doing too well. They told me to prepare myself for the inevitable."

"Oh, Rick, I'm so sorry." Lena expressed her apologies by lovingly tweaking Rick's hand.

"Don't be. He lived a long full life...and until recently, he had all his faculties. Mental *and* physical. It just makes me sad. We'd gotten so close over the years..."

After an uncomfortable moment of silence, Rick sighed, "So... enough of Andrew. What did *you* do yesterday?" Rick nudged Lena's shoulder with his own, sending an electric chill through his extremities.

Lena nudged him back. "I visited my great-grandmother. She made me lunch."

"Sounds sweet."

Lena bit her lower lip, unaware that her endearing habit was making it hard for Rick to focus. That and the fact that her fingers were caressing his palm, his stomach burned with desire. "She told me about my Nana's locket."

The locket. That prompted Rick's attention. "The locket you wear around your neck?"

Lena's head shot up. "How did you know it was this locket?" Her hands subconsciously cupped the locket around her neck.

Rick was sure Lena mentioned it the day they picnicked. "You'd mentioned it once."

Lena exhaled a sigh of relief. "Oh. Well...anyway. I just wanted to know more about where it came from."

Rick's interest was really piqued now. "So...where *did* it come from?"

"Mimi wasn't sure. She only knew that her mother wore it every day of her life...even in the end." Lena sighed. "She also said Nana always held it in her hand close to her heart." Lena smiled, aware that she still had her locket clutched in her palm. "Like I always do."

Rick chuckled. "I like when you do that."

Lena blushed.

Rick contemplated telling Lena the secret that only he...and Andrew... knew. But it was too soon. He didn't think she could hear the truth right now.

As far as Lena was concerned, she'd only met Rick when she began working with him. She had no idea the part Rick had already been playing in her life...long before she started working at the cable company.

Rick decided it'd be best to wait a bit longer. Instead, he would ask her out on another date.

While musing over his dilemma, he hadn't realized Lena had been talking. "I'm sorry, Lena, my mind was wandering. What did you just say?"

"I said, I had this odd dream last night. I think...I was dreaming about my Nana, Angelina, when she was a teenager or something. But she was with this boy Richard. According to Mimi, her father's name was Timothy. She never heard her mother mention anyone named Richard."

"Hmm." Rick's heart hammered beneath his chest again. Maybe she *would* remember. "Maybe she had a boyfriend or something before she got married. It happens." Rick hoped Lena didn't notice his unsteady breathing, brought on by her flicker of a memory, even though she hadn't quite figured it to be a recollection from her *own* past.

Lena smirked. "I know it happens, but how would I *know* that?" Lena shrugged. "I don't know. I do always have crazy dreams. I'm probably just making it up in my head." Lena hesitated. "It's just..." But she ended her thought prematurely, leaving Rick to wonder hopelessly what she had wanted to say.

He was eager though to find out. If his intuition was correct, at this moment, it may not be too early to tell her. "What, Lena? It's just, what?"

"Hmm," mumbled a baffled Lena.

"You said, it's just. It's just, what?"

"Oh." she chuckled. "It's just that I *knew* Richard. I don't know how, but I knew him. I just can't figure out from where."

Chapter Twenty-One

Rick's heart stopped. She remembered. Maybe not consciously, but some part of her...deep inside...felt the connection. It took every ounce of resolve to keep his secret to himself and not blurt it out. He wasn't sure if she was ready to hear the truth. Maybe not. This was a fragile situation and Lena, a fragile soul.

But he couldn't let the subject totally drop. "Your dreams seem like they're trying to tell you something." Rick stumbled on what to say next. "I don't know...maybe...dig deeper into them."

"Dig deeper?" Lena gasped, "Some of them are *nightmares*...I'd just rather they go away."

"Oh, Lena," a regretful Rick started. "I'm so sorry. You were talking about last night's dream. I hadn't realized you were having nightmares."

"That's okay. I may not have mentioned them to you." Lena cast her eyes downward.

Sighing, Rick moved closer to Lena and placed his hand on her leg. "What's scaring you about your nightmares?"

Lena kept her eyes down, but her foot tapped repeatedly on the ground, alluding to her anxiety.

"It's okay. If you don't want to talk about it…" Rick stood, taking Lena's hand. "Let's walk." He led them towards the edge of the lake, then circled it while they strolled hand in hand.

"Have you heard from Vince?" A curious Rick needed to know.

"No," she whispered.

"That's a good thing, right?"

"I guess." A soft whimper escaped Lena's lips.

Concerned, yet afraid of her response, Rick asked anyway, "You miss him?"

"I don't know."

"Okay, I'll drop the subject." Rick's disheartened heart dropped into his stomach.

Silence filled the air for a minute before Lena looked up at Rick. "I feel sorry for him."

Rick thought she had more to say, but she averted her eyes downward as they continued to walk. He felt a heaviness in his chest when he thought of the heartbreak he seemed to hear in her words.

The twosome had been so engrossed in their own thoughts that they hadn't realized how far they'd walked. They had entered a clearing on the opposite side of the lake. In the clearing, another stone-covered bench surrounded by overgrown berry trees and shrubs circled around them.

"Lena, we've reached the other side of the lake. I think we're late getting back to work," Rick noted.

"Oh no, I hope Dan won't be mad." Lena worried.

"I can talk with him if you'd…"

But before Rick could complete his sentence, Lena jumped in, "No!...No, thank-you. I'll just tell him I lost track of time. Please don't let him know I was with you," she pleaded.

So Lena would be facing him, Rick took her other hand in his. "Lena, I won't say anything. But…we're not doing anything wrong. Why wouldn't you want Dan to know we had lunch together?"

Lena breathed, "I guess I just feel guilty."

"For what?" Rick wondered.

"Well…I…well, I just broke up with Vince…and now…" she dropped her head. "Now I like you." Rick watched her shoulders tighten. Maybe she felt uncomfortable admitting her attraction.

With his hands still clutching Lena's hands, Rick tugged her gently toward him. Now inches apart, he peered into her brown eyes. "I like you, too." He watched a modest Lena blush and look down at the ground. With his fingertips, Rick tilted her chin back up. "Lena. It's okay to like someone else. Vince wasn't all that nice to you anyway."

Lena let out the breath that evidently she was holding.

"No one has to know yet. When you're ready...you can say something. But...I'd hate to not be able to spend time with you...unless." Rick subconsciously softened his voice. "You aren't ready to be in another relationship."

Lena hesitated. "I'm not sure."

Rick kissed her on the forehead. "Let's be friends for now then."

Relief immediately displayed in Lena's eyes and posture. "Yes. Being friends is okay."

"Well," Rick continued. "Would it be all right to invite my friend to my house this weekend,...for lunch, let's say?

"Really?"

"Yes, really." But he couldn't help himself; he leaned in and hugged her. And to his surprise, she let him. Her head fell just below his chin and her cheek rested in the hollow of his chest. The frantic beating of his heart was now probably apparent to Lena as she pressed against him. He could not slow down its pace though; he had waited years and years for this moment. This point in time where he'd be holding, in his own two arms, the love of his life.

Chapter Twenty-Two

Forty-five White Lake Road was a haven within itself. Fruit trees and a long gravel road prepared the way to a renovated old auburn-hued barn. Outlining the barn, were the most diverse multi-colored flowers and plants Lena had ever seen. Violet, yellow, orange, and red bordered the plush verdant lawn that stretched for acres and acres across the property. To the rear of the barn sat a small white farm-house adorned with a wrap-around front porch. Lena noticed that even further across the property stood a horse stable. If she wasn't mistaken, there were two horses inside.

Lena's nerves were ferociously firing as she pulled into the driveway next to the house. Rick, dressed in faded blue jeans, sage t-shirt and saddle-colored work boots, was outside watering flowers that hung in window boxes along the porch's railing.

Who was this guy? Lena wondered.

"Lena." Rick beamed, as he jumped down the stairs and raced toward his guest, giving Lena no time to wonder about him any longer. Only halfway out of her car by the time he'd reached her, Rick's open arms and illuminating smile were a welcome more appropriate for a friend who'd been gone for months than a coworker he'd just seen the day before.

But Lena relished in the warmth of Rick's hearty hug. It was fierce, yet tender. Exciting, yet safe.   Refreshing, yet achingly familiar. His embrace was a complete sentence in a one-word exclamation.

"Lena. Come on. Let me show you my house." He led her through the large oak door.

"Oh…kaay."

"You can put your purse down inside." The wooden screen door slammed shut, but Rick left the oak door open. "Want somethin' to drink?" Rick asked, already opening the refrigerator.

"Oh. No, thank you."

"All right." He took a beer out, shut the door with his foot, grabbed the bottle opener off the fridge, and opened the beer, all in one smooth beautiful movement.

"C'mon, I'll take you through the house." Lena tried to concentrate on Rick's description of each room while she followed him, but all she could focus on was how cute he looked from behind. How the pockets of his Levi's cupped his muscular back side. *Stop it, Lena,* she commanded.

Rick was describing something to her, but she'd only caught every other word. "Hmm," she mumbled, hoping he couldn't tell. Not that she wasn't interested in his house, but the warm fuzzies coursing through her body were entirely distracting. He was too darn sexy, and seeing him in his home environment was causing an uncharacteristic lustful reaction.

The house wasn't too large, so the tour took only a few minutes.

"Wanna see outside?" Lena heard Rick say. Her skin felt flush, and she hoped he couldn't see through to what she had been thinking.

"Sure," Lena tried to calm her fervor. "Can I have a glass of water first?

Rick grinned. "Of course." He reached in the refrigerator and took out a bottle of Poland Spring. "Here you go," he said, simultaneously opening it and handing it to her.

After drinking her water, she placed it on the table. "Thank you."

"No problem, let's go outside." He led her to the stables. "This is Ellie," Rick noted, pointing to a cream-colored beautiful mare, "And this here is Cal." A beautiful black horse lifted his nose as Rick petted it. "They're my best friends," he said proudly. "Have you ever ridden one?"

"A horse?" Lena gasped her answer, causing Rick's hearty chuckle. "No. Never."

"Well, maybe one day I'll show you how to ride."

Lena only nodded, afraid if she'd said yes out loud, he might actually show her how to ride. She did not want to get on top of a horse that was taller than she was.

"How 'bout a motorcycle?"

"How 'bout a motorcycle what?"

"Have you ever ridden on a motorcycle?"

What was he crazy? They're even more dangerous than a horse. "Um. No." She wondered why he was laughing again.

"Wanna go for a ride?"

"What? On a motorcycle? I don't think so."

"It's a lot of fun."

Lena didn't have the heart to let him down. "All right." She sighed.

"You don't have to, sweetie, I'm not forcing you. I just think...you'll like it, is all."

A timid Lena nodded her head and spoke under her breath, "I'll try."

"What was that? I didn't hear," he joked.

"I'll try it," she said louder.

"Great."

Holding Rick so close on the back of motorcycle felt dangerously familiar. Almost as if she knew she belonged with him. But it was too soon. Much too early in their relationship to feel this safe. And though Lena should have been elated, she became suddenly disquieted. She closed her eyes, let the sixty-miles-per-hour wind whip at her, and kept the side of her head pressed against Rick's back. Content where she was, but confused with her feelings, how could she be falling so hard...so fast?

He took her for a ride through Sparta and ended up in Warwick, New York, where finally he drove her up Barret Road. Stopping at its very highest point, the view was breathtaking. Rick pulled the bike onto the verdant open field that sat atop the unobstructed view of the serene Warwick Valley. It caught Lena's breath to see such beauty.

"You like it?" asked a satisfied Rick.

"It's magnificent."

Rick took Lena's helmet from her hands and hung it on his bike. "I come up here to unwind. The owner is a friend of mine...well, a friend of my dad's."

"The owner?..Of what?" Wondered Lena, out loud.

"The property. He owns it all. Bob owns this entire farm...even the run-down shacks on the side of the road. There's cattle too." Rick laughed.

"Wow. It's amazing here. Even the air is more fresh."

"Yeah," Rick boasted. "I'd love to build up here, but...the property's not for sale."

"You're property is just as nice."

"Thank you, but I do wish I had this view," Rick mused with a sigh.

Lena wished she could just kiss him. She knew he wanted to the other day in the park, and now she wished he'd make a move today. Up here on the mountain, her heart raced, wanting so badly to be in his arms. But her heart spoke a foreign language that her head didn't know how to translate yet. She knew it'd be wrong, her broken engagement, barely cool. Though she had been the one who had ended it with Vince, it was Lena who'd been hurt. Physically *and* mentally. Her self-esteem had been attacked, and she needed to fight her way back to a healthy well-being. Falling right into the arms of another guy would not help her to heal.

Chapter Twenty-Three

As much as Rick felt he knew Lena, his anxiety betrayed him...his usual self-composure lost, whenever he'd come close to her. She was intoxicating. Her mere presence had him fumbling like a nervous freshman starting quarterback. But he tried sobering himself with a couple of deep breaths. He must have been good at masking his feelings, because it didn't seem that Lena noticed. Considering the amount of times she'd fiddled with her locket, Rick could be sure she was just as nervous.

"Come 'ere," Rick said, simultaneously tugging Lena's hand to lead them to an old log laying on its side. He turned to face her as they sat. Lena's eyes turned into little crescents when she smiled, and Rick couldn't help himself...he leaned in and pressed his lips on her forehead, leaving them there for a brief tender moment.

"You are so beautiful," his thoughts slipped out, causing a soft pink glow on Lena's already childlike grin.

She bowed her head in chagrin and whispered, "Thank you."

"I'm sorry if I embarrassed you," Rick apologized half-heartedly, because he had meant what he said. Lena may not like compliments, but Rick knew she needed to hear them.

"That's okay," a still blushing Lena replied.

"Listen to that."

"To what?" Lena asked.

"Exactly. It's so quiet up here, you can almost sense what life was like a hundred years ago. No car engines polluting the silence. No electrical wires humming. It's as if time stood still up on this mountain."

Lena snickered as she turned her attention to Rick's Harley.

"Okay. Well, you have to get up and down this road some way...and you didn't want to take my horses." Just then, an SUV drove down Barret Road, negating Rick's claim that time stood still.

Another snicker escaped Lena.

"Yeah, yeah. I get it...but...somctimes...it just *feels* like time...at least *trickled* by, up here. The road is barely paved and if you just take a look around, you can appreciate what God intended when He created..." But Rick trailed off, afraid of alienating Lena with his corny recollections of another time.

"I get it," she uttered softly. "I'm sorry I laughed. It just seemed funny...that car zipping by while you were rambling on about...well...the non-existence of technology." She chuckled again.

Rick nudged her with his elbow.

"But, really," she continued. "It does feel..." Lena's eyes tipped up to the left, probably in search of a word. "Untouched...by time."

A sense of contentment overcame Rick. Untouched by time was exactly the way he had felt about his love for the woman sitting next to him. As if the past ninety-five years had not gone by, Rick still loved this girl... now called Lena.

"Is that why you like it up here?" Her sweet voice echoing through space sent him back in time...to that fateful day in 1917.

"Angie, sweetheart, I have to go," Richard hated saying goodbye to her. The starless night mirrored his mood. Departing for the war in the morning meant leaving behind his beloved Angelina.

"Let us run away, Richard. You cannot leave me here." She looked down at her lap, while fumbling with her locket. "Please...not with her."

He knew she was referring to the monster she called Mother. "Oh, Angie, if it were in my power to stay, you know I would. We just cannot run though. What kind of life would that be for us? And what kind of man would I be?'

Angie put her head on Richard's shoulder and sighed. "That's one of the reasons I love you so much, you know? You always do the right thing....as much as I dislike it."

He took one last drag from his cigarette, tossed it, wrapped his arm around Angie, and pulled her close, now embracing her with both arms. Kissing her on top of her head, he tried to suppress his own tears. "I will be back before you know it, Angelina. I promise." Though he tried his best to reassure Angie, his heart sunk, knowing he should have never made a promise he could not guarantee he could keep.

Angie lifted her head and took off her locket. "I want you to have this," she said, as she began pulling at the heart.

"But that is yours. Why..." Then he saw what she had intended. Angie had broken the heart locket in two.

"I put this in it last night." Richard noticed the small photograph of Angelina pressed inside the heart. "Now we will both have each other's heart," she commented, while slipping the broken heart onto a chain she pulled out of her skirt pocket. "I took this from mother's box. She will never notice."

Richard allowed her to slip the locket around his neck.

Angelina looked up at him with moist eyes. "Please return, Richard. Promise?"

Her words cut into his heart, piercing its center with the truth. Though he did not yet know his fate, the heaviness that weighed on his chest was not a good indication. "Promise," he whispered, choking back his tears, saying a silent prayer that he would, indeed, return and keep his promise to his Angie.

"Rick." Somewhere in the distance he heard his name.

"Rick." His thigh felt warm. "Rick, are you okay?" Lena asked, her hand gently squeezing his thigh.

"Oh...my goodness, Lena. I'm so sorry. I...I spaced out there for a minute." What an ass. Couldn't he have flashed back in time when he was alone, rather than while he was on a *date* with Lena. "I am so sorry."

"Oh, it's fine. I just...you looked like you were in another world...at first, I thought you were just enjoying the view, but...but then you looked kind of...sad."

"I did?" Rick had not wanted Lena to see him like that. "Um...I was just thinking is all...everything's fine." With a semi-trembling hand, he touched Lena's cheek. "Oh, Lena. I've waited a long time for you."

If the crumpled-up expression on her face indicated her confusion, then Rick had a lot of explaining to do. He knew the time had come to tell her, but he feared her reaction. Still, he held steady. It was now or never. His gut told him to go for it. The muffled thoughts in his brain, however, may have been telling him otherwise. Since his gut lay closer to his heart, he went with *it*.

"You may think I'm crazy," he began. "But, I've been searching for you all my," Rick took a deep breath, "all my life."

Baffled, she asked, "You mean metaphorically?"

"No," he said firmly. "I mean literally."

With both his hands, he reached for hers and peered straight into Lena's eyes. "I've known you, forever."

"But..."

His two fingers on her lips prevented her from finishing. "No, Lena, please. Let me finish."

"Okay."

Back to holding her hands, Rick continued to divulge their past.

"Do you believe in reincarnation?" a trepid Rick asked.

He heard a soft tut slip from her lips before she answered. "Well, I never really thought about it before. I mean, well...why?"

The lowering sun's light that glinted off the random gold specs in Lena's irises caused her eyes to appear amber, momentarily creating a blip in Rick's train of thought.

"Do *you* believe in reincarnation?" Lena countered.

Rick nodded, still apprehensive, while his stomach performed somersaults and affected his ability to speak.

"You do?" she asked.

"I do," he finally blurted. Closing his eyes and taking a reaffirming breath, he elaborated, "I do, and I believe...I've loved *you* in a past life."

Her hands pulled out from his, a deliberate move on her part, Rick thought.

"You think I'm crazy." He was worried now.

"No." The shake of her head, not at all convincing. "No, I don't."

"Do you think it's impossible?" he questioned.

Lena was nearly chewing off her bottom lip, all the while tightening her hand around her necklace. "Well, I guess not...but...even if it were possible, how...how would you remember your past life anyway?"

Rick's stomach assaults were vanishing. At least Lena seemed open-minded about it. "Some people just do. Though...you're right, most do not remember, which is why it's so hard for people to believe we can be reincarnated." He took it slow, not wanting to trounce on her already pre-conceived beliefs.

"But see," she started slowly. "I believe in Heaven, and if we *are* reincarnated, how can we go to Heaven?"

Rick let out a chuckle. "I don't have all the answers, sweetheart. I do not recall where I'd gone after my last life, but...I do believe I had at least one past life and...I believe that, in *that* life, I fell in love with...you." He searched her eyes for a reaction.

After a few moments, he heard, "Then why wouldn't I remember that?"

"I don't know...but I wish you would...remember."

Lena's eyes had that faraway look in them. He was sure he had lost her. Her smile exhibited courtesy, not sincerity, and Rick suddenly felt the urge to tell her he'd been pulling her leg about the whole thing.

He digressed. "Why don't we head back? We can get something to eat."

"Okay." Lena jumped right up, undoubtedly too eager to drop the whole subject.

Chapter Twenty-Four

Clutching Rick's backside thrilled Lena just as much on the ride back as it did on the trip up Barret Road. But Lena could not wrap her head around the whole past life theory. It didn't make sense to her. Sure, she felt a connection with Rick almost immediately, but she attributed that to chemistry, not reincarnation. As a practicing Catholic, she had been taught that souls went to Heaven...or Hell. They were not...recycled, for goodness sake.

Reincarnation was a difficult concept for her to fathom. Especially after a lifetime of believing something totally different. However, they had reached Rick's house before Lena could come up with a reasonable explanation in her mind about past lives and if they had actually existed. She laughed to herself, wondering if anyone really had a definitive answer about that.

"So, what are you in the mood for?" Rick asked, while taking Lena's helmet and hanging it on the handlebar next to his.

"Um," Lena murmured, unsure as to what context Rick was talking.

He smirked. "Lunch, Lena. What are you in the mood to eat...for lunch?" He smiled.

A warm sensation filled Lena's cheeks. Her hesitation to his question could have been misinterpreted, and she hoped he didn't assume she was thinking...sexually. Oh, she was so embarrassed.

"I got it," Rick resumed, most likely realizing how uncomfortable she felt. "How 'bout I whip us up a pizza?"

"*Whip* us up a pizza? You just whip yourself up a pizza when the whim hits?"

It was Rick's turn to blush. "Well, since we planned on you coming up here, I bought a bunch of different stuff for lunch...so, in case you didn't like something,...well, you get the picture," he trailed off.

"What else did you get?" Only out of curiosity did Lena ask, she was perfectly content with a whipped-up pizza.

"I got stuff to make subs and taco stuff and of course, I went to the bakery to get you a black and white cookie."

"You're funny."

"Well, what would you like...to eat?"

"Oh, pizza's good. I'll help you make it."

"Great. It'll be fun."

He led her into the old farm-house kitchen and showed her the pantry. After gathering all the ingredients, they met at the butcher-block counter in the center of the room and began preparing the pizza together. After Rick pressed out the dough and spread the sauce, he stood behind Lena and put his hands on her shoulders. She was slicing the mozzarella and slipped with the knife when he began massaging near her neck. Afraid he would notice that it was becoming increasingly impossible to slice the cheese, she slowed down the slicing. A pleasant chill ran through her, while the sensation of the tender movements of his fingers caused her knees to go weak. If she continued to use the knife, she was sure she'd slice a finger or two. But she did not want him to stop. It felt so...wonderful.

Rick must have noticed that she had stopped her culinary duties altogether, because, in the next moment, Rick reached around her and slowly removed the knife from her hand, placing it on the butcher-block. Lena closed her eyes, aware where he was going with this. Rick tenderly touched his lips to her neck, taking her hand and moving her to face him. When she saw his gaze lower to her mouth, she subconsciously licked at her bottom lip. He must have taken her subtle move as an invitation to kiss her, because in the next moment, he bent down and kissed her sweetly on the mouth. He didn't linger, though, moving his lips from her mouth to her nose and then her forehead. Without looking at her, he pulled her to his chest and gently stroked her hair with one hand, while pressing his palm against her lower back.

"I hope you didn't mind that," Rick whispered into her hair.

Lena assumed he was talking about kissing her. "No," she whispered into his chest, happy that he did, indeed, kiss her…and breathless because he had.

After about a half-minute hug, Rick pulled away, just enough to look Lena in the eyes. Taking her hands, he smiled at her. "I know you want to get a grasp on ...your feelings about your break-up and all, I just...had an overwhelming," he closed his eyes briefly, "desire to kiss you."

Lena offered a smile back, unsure of how to respond. She'd wanted the kiss. Hoped for it. But she also knew that diving head-first into another relationship would only put a Band-Aid over the wounds in her heart. Lena needed to figure out why she had allowed herself to be treated so abusively by Vince. Why she permitted another person to beat and belittle her was beyond her. Jumping into a romance with Rick would mask her confusion and just delay the underlying reasons for Lena's low self-worth.

So instead of saying anything, she remained silent. Rick took her lead and digressed.

"We'd better finish up on this pizza, before we end up eating it for dinner instead of lunch," Rick resigned.

****

For the second time today, Rick started something he could not finish. Or rather, Lena would not finish. First, he'd made her uncomfortable by talking about their past lives. Second, he had kissed her, knowing she wasn't ready. Damn him. Moving too fast was certainly the quickest way to alienate her. But he had wanted so badly to kiss her. Standing there in his kitchen, smelling so sweet, Lena was too enticing for Rick to resist moving nearer to her. And once near her, kissing her became inevitable. She had not resisted, either. Lena seemed to welcome his lips on hers. Yet, even though she had probably felt a connection, intuited their undeniable love for each other, he knew it wouldn't be fair to her to add another complication in her already complicated life. So he backed away, though it killed him to do so.

While the pizza browned in the oven, Rick and Lena drank iced tea on his front porch.

"So, Lena...now that you're...free to do as you please, will you be looking into the television production field again?"

Lena's eyes widened while a startled expression swept across her face. "Oh, well, I hadn't really thought about that...why?"

"I know that your heart was in television production and...I also know it was what's his

170

name," Rick still hated saying his name, "who kept
you from it, so...I...uh, just assumed."

"Oh. No. I'm happy where I am."

"Really?" Rick couldn't truly believe Lena
was happy as a PR Rep, when he knew she had
studied to be in television.

"Yes, really," Lena intoned, clearly wanting
to drop the subject.

Leaving not many permissible subjects to
discuss, Lena made it difficult for Rick to talk
about anything.

"Rick, can I ask you something?"

"Sure," Rick said, happy to talk about
anything. Any topic was better than none at all.

"What makes you believe you've actually
lived before?" Lena seemed to form her words
slowly, as if not really ready to hear the answer.

Rick proceeded with caution. "Well...my
visions, for one. As far back as when I was twelve,
I can remember seeing things that...weren't really
there," Rick paused, contemplating if he should
divulge that it was Lena's former self that he'd
envisioned. He decided against it. "People I knew,
yet had never met."

Lena nodded, probably taking in what he
had just said.

"Sporadically at first, then more frequently
as I got older...and figured out how to actually...,"
he searched for a word, "*summon* a vision."

"Summon a vision?"

Rick nodded and laughed. "Yes. I figured out that every time I lit a cigarette...that smell...kinda took me back. To where, at first, I didn't know, but...it was always the same place. Same people...familiar people," Rick smiled, thinking of a past vision of Angie. "After a while, it just became...second nature. If I wanted to slip back in time..." When Rick saw Lena's eyes growing larger by the second, he thought he'd better pull back a bit. "I'd light up. Anyway, enough about that, let's go check our pizza."

She smiled, as Rick's heart sank, an overwhelming feeling of despair coming over him. If he was not careful, he would lose Lena. Of this...he was certain.

Chapter Twenty-Five

"Hey, it came out pretty good," Lena announced, when Rick pulled the pizza out of the oven.

"And you had doubt?" he joked, as he placed it on the butcher block.

While the pizza settled, Rick poured more iced tea and set out the plates. Lena grabbed the napkins and sat down at the small circular table positioned in the window-lined alcove just off Rick's kitchen. Waiting for him to slice the pie, Lena thought how much she wanted to believe Rick's past-life proclamations. It would be cool to know someone loved her so much, that they'd come searching for her through lifetimes. But...if it was possible to be reincarnated, had Rick really come looking for her? Or was it just a fortunate coincidence? Either way, did it matter? He said he had searched for her and here they were. Was it too soon to engage in another relationship? Mixed emotions kept churning in her stomach over that question.

"Here you go, pizza a la us," Rick quipped, placing two slices in front of each of them.

"Ooh, thank you." Lena lifted a piece to her lips and blew on it before taking a bite.

"You're welcome."

"It's really good," Lena announced.

"Again, you had doubt?" Another jest, before Rick took a bite himself.

Lena let out a chuckle, but her mind was really on Rick's visions.

Her preoccupation must have been apparent to Rick, because he gave her a look of suspicion, raising one of his eyebrows. "What's on your mind?"

Lena took one long, deep breath. "You mentioned your visions...and...you said you...knew me in...the past...," Lena tapered off, unsure of what she really wanted to know, but she continued looking Rick in the eye. Her natural instinct being to avert her eyes, she didn't, knowing her need to *see* through to Rick's soul was paramount right now.

"Are you sure you want to discuss this? I mean, are you ready to hear what I have to say? I don't want you...running, before I get a chance to...capture your heart." Rick smiled, but it didn't reach his eyes. Lena could tell he was just as nervous as she.

After a moment's thought, Lena declared, "Yes, I'd like to hear this." She put her pizza down, suddenly losing her appetite.

Rick put his pizza down, too, then rested his chin on his clasped hands. "You were the girl in my visions. I was twelve when I first saw you. I remember the actual date, too. It was October tenth, nineteen eighty-six...."

Lena felt the blood drain from her face, which is probably why Rick halted his soliloquy. "What?" he asked.

"That's my birthday." She felt the words form on her lips, but she didn't hear her voice come out.

"October tenth?"

"Yes, nineteen eighty-six."

Now his face paled, while his jaw dropped. He just stared at her. "Lena," he said finally. "What time ....were you born?"

"Nine thirty-six...in the morning."

Sitting back against his chair, he sighed. "That. Is. The. Exact. Time."

"What?" a very bewildered Lena asked.

"Nine thirty-six am, the time I had my first vision. I remember, because I had just looked at my watch. So..." Rick was clearly thinking about something in particular. "Your entrance into your current life... triggered my visions. Now see, I was *meant* to find you again, Lena," smiled a now proud Rick.

Lena was...frightened, to say the least. Her innate feeling was to trust Rick. He would not lie to her. Deep down, she knew this. But his theories, or his truths, according to him, shook the very foundations in which she'd anchored her own beliefs. She was born from Heaven, a creation of God, lived one earthly life and died, returning to Heaven, with God's good grace. Reincarnation did not fit into her cycle of life.

But...what about *her* dreams? Were they visions of *her* past life?

"Rick...the girl in your visions...did she look like me?"

Shaking his head, he responded, "No, not really. There were similarities, but no, she did not look like you do now. If that's what you're asking?"

Lena nodded, "Yeah, I was. But, ok." Lena needed to know things now. "Then...how do you know... that I was her?"

"Good question," nodding, his chin still resting on his hands, Rick answered, now shaking his head back and forth. "I didn't know...at first. But...there was something about you. Something that made me stop in my tracks." He put his hands down and lightly tapped on the table. "Outwardly, I saw no real resemblance at first. That's not what stopped me. It was this intensity I felt...when I walked by you. Do you remember that day?"

Lena smiled. Of course she remembered.

"You slammed your hand in your car door."

"Yes." Lena chuckled. "I do remember."

"Well, that's when I felt it. My intuition told me it was you." Rick took a bite of his pizza.

"But you don't know for sure," Lena stated, more than asked, still afraid to accept this new realization.

"You need proof?" Disappointment set in Rick's eyes.

She let out a nervous sigh, her stomach doing its usual somersaults again. "Yea. I need proof." To actually believe all this, yes, Lena did need proof...and how on Earth, does one prove reincarnation?

****

Rick wanted to be able to give her proof. Something substantial, that would lock the truth in for her. But he didn't think he could do that. How? She'd think he was crazy. Now was not the time to think about that though. Across the table, Lena appeared green.

"Lena." Rick approached slowly. "Are you feeling all right?"

"Um...yea, just...I need to use your bathroom."

Simultaneously, they got up, and Rick led the way.

Through the closed door, he heard the unmistakable sound of Lena losing her lunch…what little she ate. "Lena, can I get you anything?" he asked through the door.

"No," she eeked out. "Actually, do you have mouth wash?"

He chuckled to himself. "Under the sink, sweetheart."

Obviously, the topic of reincarnation was too much for her. He'd rather drop the subject forever, than make her this uncomfortable.

When she finally opened the door, Rick was sitting on the floor with his back against the opposite wall.

"Were you listening?" Lena asked, aghast that he would do that.

Rick just grinned as he got up. "No. I was lost in my thoughts."

"Oh." Lena dropped her head.

"Hey. We don't have to discuss this. For all I know, I'm creating these images all on my own," he lied.

With her eyes still focused on the floor, Lena whispered softly, "I think I need to go."

Rick watched, as tears streamed down her cheek. "Lena." Rick turned her toward him, his hands, deliberately, on her shoulders. "I'm sorry. You asked. I would have never said anything. Please, don't cry." He pulled her to his chest and held her.

For two seconds.

"I need to go." Lena's eyes remained averted while she went to clear the table.

"Lena. Stop. Don't do that. If you're not feeling well, just go. Go 'head." He handed her purse to her. "I can drive you, if you'd like."

"No, I'd rather be alone"

"Okay." Sadness overwhelmed him, as he walked her to her car and said good-bye. The pressing pain in his chest increased as her car got further from his sight. He'd lost her...before he'd even had a chance to love her.

Chapter Twenty-Six

The rippling road ahead of her was near impossible to see through the rapid releasing of her tears. There was no holding them back once she turned out of Rick's drive. Lena felt ready to believe Rick. Ready to welcome the idea that reincarnation was possible, and a past life in love with Rick could have actually existed.

But the moment the contents of her stomach splashed into the toilet water, so did the future she thought she might have had with Rick. Right then and there, in Rick's bathroom, she knew. The intense upset in the pit of her stomach and the crushing pain in her heart told her so.

Lena was pregnant.

With Vince's baby.

That horrid night, when Vince forced himself on her, now came back to her as a violent replay in her mind. The highway disappearing in front of her, she tried to dry her eyes with her sleeve, afraid her blinding tears would cause a car crash.

Reaching Haledon was no easy feat, considering. But Lena stopped off at the Rite-Aid, before going home. She needed to see the proof for herself.

And she did. Lena sat on the cold green tile of her bathroom floor, unable to move. She cried until there were no more tears left to cry. Hours went by before she got up off the floor. When she finally reached her room, her bed was of no comfort, either. She lain awake, questions bombarding her mind. Lena was scared. How would she tell her parents? What did this mean for her and Vince? Was she obligated to tell him? Was she obligated to marry him now? Would her parents make her marry him? Would *his* parents make her? What would Rick think? And could she ever let herself love Rick now?

So many questions, not enough answers. What would she do? What *could* she do? Lena would have to tell her parents. But, Vince. Did he even earn the right to know? This baby wasn't conceived from his love for her. No, deliberate force was the catalyst to this conception. Vince would not see it that way. Since her parents knew nothing of his rape of her, they would not see it that way either. Unless she admitted it, finally.

At some point, Lena must have fallen asleep, because suddenly, she found herself in another time.

"Mom," twenty-five year-old Emmie began. "Why have you been so down lately? Can I help?"

"Oh Emmie, you do help, always. I've just been thinking about our life. Since your brothers and sisters have moved out of the house, I was wondering if we should take a trip somewhere."

"How can we though? I'm in a wheelchair, you do not drive and we have no money."

"Emmie, it's okay. I have enough saved up for a bus trip. I've always wanted to see the ocean. Are you up for it?"

"I am, Mom. That sounds wonderful."

Angelina had longed to see the ocean water since she was thirteen years old. A bittersweet moment that provided her joy, as well as pain. She grabbed her locket and held it close to her lips. Richard had promised to take her here. But he left, for the war, and never came back, leaving her to endure the wrath of her mother, before running away from home and into the arms of a man nearly as evil.

Her life, she could not help but think, would have turned out differently, had Richard not gone off to war. She would have married him and raised her children in a peaceful home. She would have never had the same seven children, but she would not have had to live with the guilt of sending her husband's love child off to an orphanage because his lover was too young to care for her own child. Angelina could have risen above the abuse from her mother and recovered from witnessing the brutal murder that took place when she was thirteen. If she had had the comfort and safety of a loving marriage, Angelina may have been able to salvage some of her self-esteem.

Angelina stood overlooking the big blue mass of thundering water, contemplating her life's sorrow. However, her husband was gone now and her children had families of their own. Now it was Angelina's turn. And Emmie's turn, too. To move in a more positive direction. Angie did not have much of a savings account, but she would use what she had, for annual visits to her now favorite place in the whole wide world. Seaside Heights, New Jersey.

Lena awoke, almost comforted by her latest dream, a dream she already remembered having, but in not so much detail. Mimi had told stories of Aunt Emmie and how she was diagnosed with Multiple Sclerosis when Emmie was only thirteen years old. Lena was told, that to Nana, Emmie was everything, and the two of them were inseparable. Nana had realized that, though all of her other children were independent, Emmie would never be able to manage on her own. Blind and wheelchair-bound, Emmie had only lacked physically. Her mind was sharp and heart, kind. Nana made it her life's work to care for Emmie. Lena had learned, through stories, about the summer bungalow that her great-great-grandmother rented each year in her later years. The fond memories of Summers spent in Seaside Heights were shared over and over, even by her own mother.

What suddenly occurred to Lena was, though she could have dreamt Nana's stories, based on her knowledge of them, why could she *feel* Nana's thoughts and feelings of Richard? And, why, every time she thought of Richard, Lena thought of Rick?

A pang in her heart alerted Lena to her current situation. Living in a dreamland was not going to help her make immediate, life-altering decisions. She needed to buck-up and face this dreaded reality head on. Lena needed to think. Since her dream about the Jersey shore was still fresh in her mind, Lena decided to take a drive down to Seaside Heights for the day. A long drive down the Garden State Parkway, while listening to *Daughtry*, would help her organize her thoughts. Music did that for her. It possessed the ability to weave itself deep inside the crevices of her mind, helping to connect it with her soul. Once housed firmly within her, a song could provide a clearer vision and a confirmed solution. Music was her bloodline, and today she would allow it to feed her veins.

Reaching the Seaside boardwalk in about an hour and a half, Lena had felt lighter – the songs, from her Daughtry CD, resonating throughout her body, mind and soul. Since it was now nearing summertime, there were plenty of stands open.

Lena took advantage of her pregnancy hunger and divulged in the zeppole, pizza, waffles and ice cream and fudge. Oh, the fudge. Lena loved boardwalk fudge, especially from Laura's Fudge Stand. Laura's Fudge was situated near the beloved carousel that held so many memories for Lena. She could not really discern why the carousel had meant so much, but it did. She bought her fudge and sat on the red painted bench that looked on at the old antique merry-go-round.

As Lena allowed the soft rich chocolate fudge to saturate her taste buds, it released, in her mind, a mystical image. A vision, so supernatural, she could not believe her own eyes. Riding the carousel was her great-great-grandmother Angelina as a young girl. And with the young Angelina, was another girl. A familiar child with straight brown hair, brown eyes, and an unmistakably recognizable smile. Lena's smile. The other rider on the carousel was Lena as a twelve-year old. An uninhibited and innocent young Lena looked to have not a care on her tiny shoulders compared to the slack-shouldered and burdened young Angelina. Although in Angelina's eyes, Lena witnessed a flash of a glimmer. A quick glint in her eye that lasted only a second but sent a message, so clear, to the present Lena, that she could not help but understand.

Lena needed to take control of her life. She needn't let one situation define or inhibit her. What she took from this surreal experience was the message from her younger self to be the happy person she once was. And the younger version of her Nana sent the message of hope. If Lena could not let her burdens destroy her, she would find hope for a better future. Could that be why Lena kept dreaming about her Nana? Was Nana trying to send a message to Lena? Or...was there another reason for her visions of Angelina? An unexplainable explanation.

Chapter Twenty-Seven

Lena's attempt to confide in her parents about her pregnancy was not going to be a smooth endeavor. Pulling up to her parents' house after her drive home from the shore, Lena's whole body tensed while her heart sank to the pit of her stomach. Parked in front of the antique hitching post in front of the Giordano's house was a large black Mercedes S600. Vince Battaglia's parents' car. A bad sign, indeed.

Approaching the porch steps slowly, Lena did a quick sign of the cross praying God would give her the courage to see her through the evening. The door creaked as she edged it open, causing a slight jump in her already over-exerted heartbeat. Lena closed her eyes in an effort to gather more fortitude. Seated at the large dining room table at the far end of the parlor were Mr. and Mrs. Battaglia, Lena's parents, and Vince, whose scornful expression triggered another bout of nausea for Lena. Before hurling all over her mother's designer carpet, Lena ran for the bathroom, tossing her purse on the couch. What a way to enter a room, Lena thought. Nothing subtle about running to the bathroom to vomit. Would she be able to lie if Vince confronted her about it? She'd wanted to talk to her parents about her pregnancy privately, not in front of the Battaglias. And certainly not in front of Vince. Did he even have any rights to her baby? He raped her for goodness sake. But then again, they were engaged, and in his mind he had every right to have sex with her.

When did life get so complicated? Lena was only twenty-five and a half years old; this was supposed to be the prime part of her life – experiencing new things, enjoying a wild career – where did it all go wrong? Listening to Vince. That's where it all went wrong. Agreeing to turn down the production assistant position in New York City, because Vince had instructed her to do so, was her first mistake. Accepting his marriage proposal was the second.

Lena swooshed mouthwash around in her mouth, then washed her face. The splashing of the cool water on her face was a well-needed energy boost. Hopefully she could hold it together in front of the Battaglias.

"What the fu...?"

"Vince," Mrs. Morella scolded her son of thirty-one years when he responded abusively to Lena's return entrance into the dining room.

"No. I wanna know. What's going on with you?" An angry Vince addressed Lena. "You break up with me, then you're gone this entire weekend. Where were you? With your boyfriend?"

"Vince, stop," his mother again commanded.

Jules held her hand out for Lena to sit next to her.

"So what is it, Lena, you pregnant? ...With your boyfriend's baby?"

"Vince," both sets of parents exclaimed in unison.

"Vince." Lena finally spoke up. "It's not...like that."

"Ah," he yelled. "You *are* pregnant, goddammit."

Lena bowed her head, wondering how Vince picked up on it so quickly. "Yes," she whispered, but soon found her voice. "I don't have a boyfriend though, Vince. It's yours." And suddenly, looking at him felt dirty and she could no longer stand to be in the same room with him.

Before she could turn to walk out, she caught the expression on Vince's face. Like the devil getting away with murder, his shit-eating grin caused a fury so strong within Lena, that she could not ignore him. "You can wipe that grin off your face, Vince." His name tasted like hot vomit on her tongue. "You know how I got pregnant." She didn't care that their parents were there, she needed to get this out once and for all. "Or did you forget that you forced yourself on me against my will?"

Gasps were heard at the table, but Lena kept her gaze on Vince, after verbally slapping him across the face.

"What?" Frank and Mr. Battaglia said simultaneously, as Frank leapt across the table to grab Vince by the neck.

"Frank," Jules snapped. "Get down."

Frank did, but he then bolted around the table and punched Vince in the face. Vince, set to repay a punch for a punch, was intercepted by his father. "Vince," Mr. B. said. "Is this true?"

"She's my friggin fiancé, I shouldn't have to ask." Vince was pissed.

The twisted face on Mr. B spoke of shame, plain and simple. His son had clearly embarrassed and tarnished the Battaglia's reputation. "You *always* have to ask. *Always.*" Mr. B. was out the door, apparently too ashamed to be in the same room with his son.

"Lena." Jules strained to remain calm and turned toward her seated daughter, placing her hand on Lena's trembling thigh. "Did he really...force," the words, clearly difficult for Jules to utter, "did he really?" Jules cried, unable to resist her own emotions.

Nodding, Lena cried along with her mother. "I'm sorry I didn't tell you, Mom, I shoulda..."

"Oh, fuck this Lena, you were my fiancé. You didn't want to fool around. I *had to* force it in order to get any."

"Oh Vincent," Mrs. Battaglia cried. "How could you?"

"Frank." Lena and Jules had only realized, when Frank walked back into the room, that he'd disappeared momentarily. But he wasn't happy.

"You. Are. A. Monster." Her furious father grabbed Vince by the collar again. "I'm not going to hit you this time, I called the police. Forcing yourself on my daughter is a crime. They'll be here any..."

As if Frank somehow cued the sound effects, the sirens blared outside.

"No. Frank. Please. You didn't," Mrs. Battaglia pleaded. "Oh Frank, please, you can't do this, please, it'll ruin us."

"Ruin you? What about my daughter? Now she has a pregnancy to deal with. You don't think this will ruin her?" Frank snapped.

A fleeting, empathetic twinge coursed through Lena's veins. Mrs. Battaglia's concern for her reputation, rather than her son's well-being, was one of the reasons Lena had found it so hard to let go. Vince's pathetic family caused a pitying tug at Lena's heart, often softening her resolve so much, that she'd forget his misgivings. But not this time. She needed to stay strong. His upbringing was no excuse to behave in such an animalistic fashion.

His brutality towards her was wrong…regardless of his lack of parental love and guidance.

Before Lena had finished her thoughts, the policemen were in the house handcuffing her ex-fiancé, while Mrs. Battaglia cried tears of shame in the palm of her hands, and Jules held her crying daughter on the couch. Mr. Battaglia was back, evidently receiving the news of his son's arrest during the time he was gone.

Mr. B. whispered something to the officer.

"I'm sorry, Al," the officer responded to Vince's dad's whisper. "We have to take him in. We'll get a statement from both parties, we'll set bail, and we'll have Vince released by morning, latest."

Mr. B. shook his head and turned his attention to Lena's father. "Frank, you can't press charges. How much?"

"What? You think this is about money?" Frank was furious. "This is about *your* son committing a crime, plain and simple, Al."

"If it's not about money, then why bother? Abort the kid; shove the whole thing under the rug. You bring this to court, it's not just my son who gets hurt. You think your daughter's not going to be affected?"

"She's affected already...you know what, my lawyer will get in touch with you. I'm done." Frank threw his hands up in the air.

"Sir," the officer interrupted, attending to Frank. "We do need to get a statement from your daughter. Can you bring her down tonight?"

Lena watched her father's somber nod. Her breaking heart was crumbling even more knowing she was the cause of her parents' sorrow. If only she had put a stop to Vince's abuse long ago. Why she hadn't, she could not say...but now... it was time.

Chapter Twenty-Eight

Lena was having a hard time falling asleep. After she gave her statement at the station, she went home to her empty apartment and cried. Luckily for her, Jules and Frank were understanding and assured her that they would be fine, as long as they knew *she* would be. Lena refused their request that she stay in her old room, but she was now regretting that decision. At least in her parents' presence, her thoughts were of *their* pain and remorse. Here, alone... in the silence... all she could think about was the crashing of a relationship, that now could never be.

Yesterday had been a perfect beginning to an exciting new courtship.

Today would be the end.

Too cowardly to break the news about her pregnancy to Rick, Lena wrote him a letter instead. The words would come out jumbled anyway, if she were to tell him to his face. And she didn't think she could look him in the eyes and tell him goodbye...forever.

Dear Rick,

I am so sorry that I am not telling you this face to face. I wish I could be a stronger person and face my challenges like an adult, but I am not. I try sometimes, but mostly, I fail.

Anyway, please find it in your heart to forgive me for telling you this way. I'm pregnant. And it's Vince's...from that night he left me beaten in my own home. I should have never let it get that far, I know. But, I did and I have to live with it. Yesterday was so wonderful, being with you. The reason I left so abruptly was, that, while I was in your bathroom, I'd realized what had happened. It all came back to me. That night Vince busted in my apartment. All the upset stomachs I've been having. I just knew. And I just had to leave you, before you had to watch me cry...again. Before you had to pick up the pieces of my shattered life. You don't deserve that. I'm not sure which way my life is going right now, but I know I cannot drag you into it.

If you truly believe in reincarnation, Rick, and you truly believe you've come back for me in this life, then, maybe in the next life, you can come look for me again. I am so sorry. I will miss you.
Love, Lena

She sealed the envelope, stamped it, and put it in her mailbox for the postman to pick up in the morning. A call in sick to work was inevitable this week. Avoiding Rick would be too difficult, she would have to let him adjust to the news and hope he'd be over it when she returned next week.

Lena didn't think she would ever get over Rick. Like the moon pulls the tide, Lena had been drawn to Patrick Murphy from the beginning. Her soul seemed to awaken from the moment she saw him in the parking lot. Eliminating that magnetic force from her life almost seemed dangerous. As if she suddenly would...stop existing. But she needed to take that risk. How could she expect him to love a child that wasn't even his? A child who she was finding difficult to believe was even hers.

Would Lena be able to love this baby? Maybe she'd resent him, memories of its conception weighing too much to turn the bitterness away. If she could not predict her own feelings to this new child, how could she expect Rick to be okay with it? And she would not hold the burden of his emotions as well as her own.

Lena had contemplated abortion...fleetingly. That decision would only open up a new set of emotional concerns, and she knew herself well enough to know that abortion was not an option. Her only option was to put Rick in her past...and raise her baby on her own... with the help of her family.

****

Lena hadn't been at work on Monday, so Rick figured she was still not feeling well. Her phone had gone to voicemail, but still, Rick hadn't thought much about it. Worry inched slowly from Rick's heart to his brain, but when her cubicle stood empty again on Tuesday, his worry turned to a deep concern. Again, an animated message greeted his call to her. Deciding on his way home from work to take a quick shower and head back down to Haledon, he was stopped short by the letter in his mailbox. Her handwriting in black and white on the envelope caused a passing tremble in his hands. The overwhelming grief that washed over him when he read the first few words burned through his chest like hot coals under his feet. He dropped to his seat, blown by the words that followed.

He sat there unable to move. The words, running into each other, as he read them over and over, until they were one big watery mess. Was she really saying goodbye? Did she really think he'd walk away from her when she needed him most? Even if she had no recollection of who Rick had been in her past, she should know enough about Rick in this lifetime to realize he'd *insist* on taking care of her. Hadn't he told her as much through his actions? First, he flies off the handle at that ass of a boyfriend of hers when he spoke disparagingly to her in front of everyone. Then, going on a hunch that she was in trouble, Rick shows up at her apartment, only to realize his intuition was correct. He had held her for hours while she cried herself to sleep, yet now she doesn't want to drag him into her broken life? Too late. He's already there. Can't she tell, all he wants to do is protect her and take care of her? There was no way in Hell he'd let her walk away. Lena needed him...and he needed her. Mostly, he needed her to need him. Not that he wanted her dependent on him. Rick wanted her to need *him* as the missing piece in her life. New baby or not...he would not let her get away.

His shower went forgotten. After letting his sick stomach settle a second, he grabbed the keys off his counter and took off to rescue his distressed damsel. He was going to see her through this. Rick would not watch Lena suffer in martyrdom. Not in this lifetime.

Chapter Twenty-Nine

The echoing vibration of the doorbell ringing over and over caused the sensation of a vice forcing her temples together. He wouldn't go away. When the car door slammed, she went to the window and watched him stride up her walk. A migraine, already setting up camp in her head, became inflamed by the continual chiming of the bell.

Why wouldn't he just leave? Lena thought. She'd mailed Rick the letter so she wouldn't have to talk to him face to face. Now here he was, relentlessly ringing her doorbell and not getting the hint. She did not want to talk with *anyone,* especially Rick. How could she look him in the eye now that she had someone else's child inside of her? It'd be emotionally impossible for her to endure it. So badly did she want her relationship with Rick to get more serious, but now...she'd ruined that chance. Lena wasn't about to withstand prolonging the inevitable – she could never be with Rick Murphy without feeling pangs of remorse for tainting their courtship before it'd even had a chance to begin.

The ringing stopped. When Lena peered out the window she could not see him, but his Jeep could still be seen in the lot. From her view at the window, she could not tell if he was sitting in his car or not. But at least he'd stopped pressing the bell.

Lena collapsed onto the couch and cried knowing it would make her migraine worse, but she was unable to help herself. In such a short amount of time, Rick had become such an important person in her life. Now, he wouldn't even be a part of it.

The blaring of the sirens outside disrupted Lena's crying spell long enough for her to take a look out the window. The cop cars were parked in front of her apartment – red and blue LEDs lighting up the dusk on Barbour Street. Just then, her doorbell rang again…this time, with a handful of hard raps against the door.

"Ma'am. Open up if you can hear us. It's the Haledon PD," a gruff voice commanded, causing Lena to tremble in fear.

Oh my goodness, she thought. *What did I do? Maybe it's about Vince. Oh my God, what did he do?* Instead of opening the door for the officer, she was frozen in her thoughts.

"Ma'am," the officer demanded again, more forcefully. "If you can hear me, open up, otherwise, we're coming in, ma'am."

Holy Crow, they're coming in? How? Lena forced herself to move. "Right there," she rasped. "I'll be right there." She tried again with a stronger voice. Wiping her eyes with her sleeve, she patted down her hair, tucked her bangs behind her ears, and descended the stairs to open the door.

"Miss Giordano?" the Haledon cop asked after Lena opened the door. "Are you all right, ma'am?"

Shocked, she could only nod. Her fragile stomach, now in knots, added to the nausea and the migraine that the pregnancy had already caused.

"We got a call that no one had heard from you in a few days. We know you're Vince Battaglia's fiancée. He was let out on bail and we were worried that he...well..." The cop trailed off, probably unsure of what he should say.

Lena shook her head and swallowed the lump that had formed in her throat. "No. I'm fine. I...haven't heard from Vince."

"Great."

"Who...who...who called you?" Lena wondered, apprehensively questioning the officer.

"A Mister..." He looked down at his notepad.

"I did," a voice, from the other side of the porch, announced.

Immediately whipping her head around, she gasped, "Rick?"

"Yes, Lena, me. I was worried about you, so I called the police."

"Miss Giordano," the cop interrupted, "if you're all right, we'll be on our way."

"Oh, yes...yes, of...of course...I'm fine. Um, you didn't like...alert my parents or anything...did you?"

"No, Miss, we came here first, just in case you were in trouble. Well, take it easy and...answer your phone and your door once in a while, so you don't scare your friends."

Lena feigned a chuckle. "Right, sorry."

"Why?" Incredulous, she questioned Rick once the officer took off. "Why on Earth, would you call the police?"

With two long strides, he was inches from Lena. "Did you really think I wouldn't find a way to get to you? I've traveled an entire lifetime to find you. You think someone else's baby is going to keep me away?" Rick peered deep into her eyes, so much so, it made Lena tingle just a bit. Plus, it made her nervous to have him intruding into her soul, which she knew he was trying to do. "Well, think again," he finished, vexed by her actions to exclude him from her life.

"Go home, Rick." She couldn't face him. Turning to go back up the stairs, attempting in vain to close the door on him, he pushed it open and took her elbow. Guiding her in and shutting the door behind him, Rick pulled her into his arms and carried her up to her apartment.

"Put me down. I can walk." Her weak demand, unconvincing, he still cradled her in his arms. "Please, put me down," Lena commanded more forcefully this time, convincingly enough that he set her down once they reached her living room.

Once up on her own two feet, she stomped one of them. "How dare you call the police? Every single one of them knows my father...and worse..." Frustrated, she squeezed her temples, the migraine letting her know it was still there in full force. "Vince's family is going to find out now." She gave a soft pound with her fist to the top of her old television set. "Damn-it," she whispered aloud.

"I'm sorry," said a grinning Rick.

"What? Why are you smiling like that?"

"I'm not smiling," he said, smiling.

"This isn't funny, Rick. You called the cops...because I wouldn't let you in." Her voice pitched an octave too high out of sheer frustration.

Toning down his grin, he moved forward. "I'm not laughing, sweetheart, not at all." He proceeded closer to Lena but she backed away. A frown instantly replaced his grin. Lena felt bad, but she really did not want him in her apartment. Staying put where he was, Rick opened and closed his mouth a few times, as if to speak, before finally saying, "I was only smiling, because I liked your...pluckiness tonight...you've got spunk. I haven't seen that before."

"Wait, what? What does that have to do with anything? Uggh." Thwarted in her intention to avoid Rick, Lena threw her hands up in the air and plopped on the couch annoyed. Flopping her head against its back, she stared at the ceiling.

Cautiously, Rick moved toward the couch to sit at the opposite end, obviously defeated in his own original intentions. What they were, Lena wasn't sure yet.

"Lena." A noticeably guarded Rick proceeded slowly. "I received your letter this afternoon."

Lena remained attentive to the ceiling, as plain and white as it was.

"I'm sorry this has happened to you. You did not deserve what that man did to you. But I won't let you face this alone."

As hard as she tried to keep her focus off of Rick, Lena found it increasingly difficult. Why would he want to drag himself into her problems? What was in it for him? Motioning with her eyes first, Lena then turned to look at Rick. "Why?" The soft question fell from her lips, along with a tear from her eye.

"Why won't I let you face this alone? Because I love you. Plain and simple."

"You...love me? You haven't even known me...oh, yeah, that's right...you knew me in a *past* life," she mocked, hating herself for her sudden sarcasm.

"Yes, I did." Rick wasn't swayed, or if he was, he didn't appear to be. "But even so, you ever hear of love at first sight?"

"Hmmph." Such a child she was.

"You're not going through this alone, Lena. Whether you like it or not, you're stuck with me."

Chapter Thirty

Rick was adamant about his declaration. Lena would not go through this pregnancy alone. Whatever she decided to do about it, he'd be there right by her side. Rick would raise and love her baby as his own...because any part of Lena, was a part of him. It didn't matter that his mere presence made her angry. The world made her angry, and he didn't blame her. For so long she tried to be nice, seeing the good in that evil excuse for a human being she called her fiancé. And this is how she's repaid? No, Rick did not blame her one bit for being angry.

He *was* scared for her though. Lena had already formed a hard shell around her heart. A shell that hadn't been there before. Circumstances like this could definitely change people, and he feared for Lena, her childlike nature. One could only endure so much in one lifetime, before the heart hardened. In Lena's case, her soul had already suffered through an entire lifetime, and history had now begun to repeat itself. One soul can only take so much before it shows signs of wear and tear. Her recent, bitter derision was one of those signs. Though against her character to be disparaging, Rick understood why she had suddenly fallen prey to cynicism. Vince insensitively stole something so precious from her – her virtue – and now, she would have to live with that reminder for the rest of her life. No, Rick could not blame her for building a wall. He'd be damned, though, if he didn't attempt to knock it down. He would not leave her alone again. Not anymore.

Fighting the urge to come on too strong again, Rick sat silently as he watched another tear drop from her left eye. He could tell she attempted to suppress them, but more tears would follow. Of that, he was sure. Sullen and ill-tempered, Lena seemed to prefer silence over Rick's company, so Rick decided to give her some time to sulk. He went into the kitchen and made two cups of coffee...using her fancy coffee machine. Taking his mug with him, he sat at her tiny table for two, leaving Lena alone for a few moments. Rick hated to alienate her; it wasn't his intention to do so when he came knocking at her door. But the moment he'd opened his mouth, Lena had taken offense to him. He wouldn't take it personally, though. She just needed some time.

"Why are you sitting in here?" Lena uttered softly from the kitchen doorway.

"I'm giving you space," he answered quietly as well. Rick could see the thoughts forming in Lena's head while she stood there apparently puzzled.

"Then why not leave?" Though her hands were placed dramatically on her hips, Rick heard uncertainty in her voice.

"Now why would I do that?" Attempting to refrain from jumping out of his seat to hug her, knowing she needed one, he sipped his coffee while awaiting her response. Though *Rick* knew Lena needed a warm embrace, *Lena* didn't know it yet, being so angry and all. He would just wait until she was ready.

"Because... I told you I didn't want you here," she sassed, yet remained in the doorway, a clear indication of actions speaking louder than words.

"However," Rick began slowly. "I think you could use a friend."

He didn't think her shoulders could slump any lower than they already were, but he was wrong. Her facial expression had drooped right along with them.

"I don't need anybody." Her words were inaudible, but Rick knew exactly what Lena said and knew exactly what she meant. She was ready for that hug.

"Lena." Pushing his chair from the table, Rick stood. "Everybody needs somebody." He took two steps to the doorway, put his hands on her shoulders and pulled her close. Holding her while she cried against his chest, his heart picked up speed rapidly. With his chin on her head, Rick closed his eyes and let Lena weep while he smoothed her tresses with the palm of his hand.

After several minutes of hugging in the kitchen doorway, Lena broke the embrace. "What am I going to do, Rick?"

He took her by the hand and brought her to the table. Pulling the chair out for her, Rick motioned for her to sit, then set a cup of coffee in front of her. "It might be a little cool by now," he said, before sitting down himself.

Lena's head, cradled in her hands, caused her words to sound mumbled, so Rick almost missed it when she cried, "I've gotten myself into such a mess."

"*You* did no such thing. This whole thing is *not* your fault at all. You need to remember that, sweetheart."

"But I should have walked away...the first time I knew what he was capable of," she said in admonishment. "I'm just so..."

"Stop," he bade. "You're beating yourself up and it's not going to do you any good. We'll get through this...together."

Rick knew he was oversimplifying her whole ordeal, but he wanted to put her at ease and really did not know what else to do. As old as he was, he lacked experience in actually dealing with serious issues, while Lena's poor soul seemed to be a magnet to them.

"Why? Why do you want to help? I...I just don't understand."

"What don't you understand, Lena? I love you. You may think it's too soon, but I do, nevertheless. I cannot just turn away from you and...what? Forget you ever existed?" Rick couldn't understand how Lena could not see that.

She just stared at him, then at the table...and shook her head.

"Lena." Noticing Lena's hands on the table, Rick gently tugged at them. "If you want to keep this baby, I will help you raise it. If you don't, I will be there through that as well. I promise."

He could tell by the look in her eyes that she wasn't sure if she should trust him. "Lena, I know I have to earn your trust. I wouldn't expect anything less. But in time, I'm sure you will see that I am a man of my word."

But he still saw doubt on her face, and when he looked deep into her eyes, where he could catch a glimpse of her soul, he knew somewhere deep within her, Lena knew that Rick was *not* a man of his word. He had failed her once before. And it would not be easy to earn her trust.

Chapter Thirty-One

"Are you done with your coffee?" Rick digressed.

"Oh. Yeah. Sorry. I...kinda just went off into another world there for a second."

He laughed, got up, and put their mugs in the sink. "Let's see if there's a movie we can watch."

Lena could not explain what she had felt when Rick advocated being a man of his word. Oddly and for no reason at all, she did not believe him. The strange thing was, he had always been nothing but a gentleman and never gave her any reason not to be able to trust him.

"How's this?" Rick asked of the channel he landed on while flicking. "*It Could Happen to You.* It's one of my favorite movies."

A stunned Lena chuckled. "*This* is one of your favorite movies? Isn't it a chick-flick?" She giggled, surprising herself of being able to feel anything other than dread.

"Yes, it *is* one of my favorite movies...and who said it's a chick-flick?"

She shrugged. "Well, I like it too."

"Good. Then we'll watch it."

Rick sat at the opposite end of the couch, but Lena wanted to be closer to him. Despite the curious feeling she'd had before, she did like him. And she longed to be near him regardless. Inch by inch she maneuvered closer, but Rick reached for her and pulled her close before she had even made it to the other side of the couch. "C'mere," he'd said.

Lena blushed.

Nestled between the crook of his arm and his shoulder, Lena drifted off while watching the movie. During her sleep, though, a different scene unfolded in her mind

"Angelina. You come inside right this minute," Agnes shrieked. "Proper ladies do not sit on their front steps leering at boys. You get inside now. Otherwise, I will beat the living daylights out of you."

"Yes, Mother," Angelina answered, but *thought,* proper ladies do not beat the living daylights out of their daughters. *Angelina did not want to go inside. Content to sit out on the steps and watch Richard set the pop out on the curb, Angelina took her time going upstairs. It made her happy to watch Richard take the pop cases off the hand truck and stack them out on the sidewalk. On lucky days, Angelina's mother would get so drunk, she would have no clue what Angelina was up to. She'd sit outside until dusk just to get a glimpse of Richard putting the unsold cases back on the hand truck to bring in before his father closed up shop.*

"*Angelina,*" *came another bellow from her mother, today not being one of those fortunate nights for Angelina. Tonight her mother was just drunk enough to be wicked. Angelina caught Richard looking back at her as she reluctantly stood to go inside. She knew what Richard was thinking;* he knew what was about to happen. *Everyone knew what happened in the Mancini home, yet no one did anything to stop it. The whole town turned a blind eye to crazy drunken Agnes.*

Angelina, one slow step at a time, ascended the stairs to her apartment. An inebriated Agnes stood at the top, a wooden ruler in her hand.

"*Mama, please, I am so sorry. I just wanted to finish the chapter I was reading?*" *Angelina pleaded – in vain, she knew, but attempted to stop her mother anyway.*

"*Who are you fooling, Angelina? You were gawking at that delivery boy. Whores do that. You are turning into a whore, child.*"

"*No, Mama, no, I am not.*" *Holding back her tears felt like glass crumbling in her throat.*

But it was too late. Angelina knew Agnes' mind was set. She held the ruler sideways and started slicing her daughter's arm with it.

"*Mama,*" *Angelina winced, no longer able to hold back the tears.* "*Please.*"

Agnes whipped her with the ruler again. Though Angelina attempted to run, Agnes caught her and wrapped her again, this time slashing the back of her daughter's neck. Going at her again,

Agnes struck her daughter's cheekbone, slicing the corner of Angelina's eye and leaving a bleeding gash across her face. "Now get in your room and do not come out." Agnes staggered away, leaving Angelina to care for her own wounds.

The next day, Angelina escaped for school before her mother woke up. Already outside arranging the soda pop cases, Richard called out to Angelina, "Hey, Angie," he yelled from across the street.

Embarrassed by her appearance, Lena only waved, leaving her head down. Her face even worse this morning than last night, she couldn't bear for Richard to see her, so she kept walking, hoping to dissuade him from coming over. It hadn't helped.

"Angelina?" Crossing the street to greet her, his voice held concern.

Her gaze remained downward while she fussed with her bonnet, in another attempt to thwart conversation. "Umm...I am running late this morning, I have to go." She picked up her walking pace, hating every minute of deceiving the boy she loved. The tug on her sleeve slowed her down.

"Agnes hit you again," Richard remarked. "I will kill her." Gently touching his hand to her marred face, he positioned himself in front of her.

"She was drinking again," Angelina whispered, her head still down. "She did not mean it."

"You are always defending her, Angelina. She should not be hurting you like this." The back of his fingers caressed her wounds.

"I know, but it really is not that bad."

"Yes, Angie, it is that bad."

"Really, Richard, I can handle her. Please, do not spend any more time worrying about this...please." But Angelina knew he would not stop until he could put an end to the beatings. Which she knew was an impossible feat.

"Well, I will worry. We need to get married, Angelina. I can take you away from her," Richard said with conviction.

Angelina scoffed, *"She will never allow it, I'm only thirteen, Richard."*

"So, we will do it without her consent. I am sure my father knows someone who would marry us."

"Again, I am only thirteen, *Richard. Thirteen."*

"No matter. We love each other. What does your age have to do with it?"

But age had *everything* to do with it. Lena knew this, because, before waking fully from her dream, she had caught a different glimpse. Their goodbye... on the front steps. Richard was old enough to be drafted into the war, not long after his proposal of marriage. He left. And Angelina, unmarried yet, would never see him again.

"Hey, sleepyhead," Lena heard upon waking.

"Sorry I fell asleep," she murmured, sitting upright, trying to shake herself out of her sleepy stupor.

"Oh, don't apologize, you needed it." Rick stroked the back of Lena's hair.

"What time is it?"

"After two."

"In the morning? Oh my goodness. I'm so sorry. And you have to go to work tomorrow...today..." Lena stood, figuring Rick would want to leave. He just sat there, elbow on the sidearm, chin resting on his knuckles. "Don't you need to leave?" she wondered.

"Would you like me to leave?"

"Umm." No, she did not want him to leave. It was comfortable with him near. "I...guess not." She furrowed her brow, surprised she just told a man she really hadn't known long, that she'd like him to stay...the night. "But what about work?"

"I'll go in late. I'm the manager, it'll be fine. What about you? Are you missing again?"

"Yeah, I called out for the week. I know it's bad. I haven't even had the job long, I'm sure it doesn't look good. I just...there's just too much going on." Lena sat back down on the couch, the opposite end from Rick, and put her feet up, wrapping her arms around her knees. "Everything is so messed up, Rick." Trying her best to suppress her tears again, she couldn't help it. A stray tear tickled her cheek.

"What's messed up, Lena? You're pregnant. Obviously...you want to keep it." Lena heard the question in his voice, even though he seemed to try to keep it a statement.

The pull in her chest reminded her that she was not one-hundred percent sure about her decision to keep the baby. "I...I think so. It's just...this is not where I wanted to be. I wanted so much more," she cried.

"Like what, sweetheart?" Rick still sat at his end of the couch, cool and collected, while Lena sat frazzled, admiring his self-possession. She'd seen his temper just that once with Vince, yet he otherwise always seemed contained. Lena admired that.

As her foot rhythmically tapped on the couch, she thought about Rick's question. Not that she didn't know the answer. She knew it well. Lena had just not said it out loud to anyone. Not since before she'd turned down her first production job. "I...just...I wanted so badly to work in television...not here...in P.R...I could have started y'know. If I only put my foot down and stood up to Vince. Now...with a baby...a child to raise...now I'll never get there." Lena looked at Rick, who'd been watching her. Listening to her. He seemed so interested in what she had to say that she continued her rambling. "I know this seems so selfish, but I'm only twenty-five. I'm not ready to be a mother. I wanted to...I don't know, make music videos, movies, television shows...something...like that." Lena trailed off, tired of complaining.

For about a whole sixty-seconds, Lena and Rick sat silent, staring at each other. She, on one end of the couch, he, with one foot on the floor, one leg bent on the seat cushion, sitting on the other end. Lena figured Rick was waiting to see if she was done talking, before he responded to her rambling pity-party.

"Well," he finally started. "You can't go back and do it over, we all wish we could. But you're *only* twenty-five. A baby doesn't have to be the end. Take one day at a time, Lena. First things first. If being in television is what you want, you'll get there...if *you* make it happen. Right now though, let's get you through this ordeal. Decisions do not have to be made overnight."

Lena shook her head. "You make it seem so simple."

"No I don't. I just want you to face what's in front of you without boggling your mind with what could've been. When...it still can be."

Lena took a moment to respond, "Were you always this smart?"

Rick laughed. "I am not smart. I'm just able to see your life objectively...sort of,...which you can't. That's all...look, it's getting late. Why don't you get me a pillow and a blanket? I'll sleep on your couch, and you can go to bed and get some sleep."

Lena just then remembered her nightmare and did not want to go to sleep. "Oh, um, sure, I'll get you a pillow and...Rick? Can I ask you something?"

"Sure," a smiling Rick answered.

"Was your name...um...Richard?"

Chapter Thirty-Two

Rick stilled.

She remembered.

He had to be careful, so not to frighten her away. He'd longed for this day. The moment he would share his memories of the woman who had taken hold of his soul so many years ago.

"As in, was my name Richard in...my past life?" he asked, cautious and slow, afraid of the direction the conversation could take.

Two nods. "Yes." Her answer, as uncertain as his question, informed him that she was equally as nervous.

"Yes. My name was Richard."

Her breaths appeared more labored as her chest began a rapid rise and fall. The sudden remoteness of her eyes frightened Rick, but he soon realized she was seeing something. Something not here... but in another time. Lena's expression mimicked what Rick had felt when he'd been traveling somewhere in another time. He'd read online that some would call it *Astral Travel*, but he knew it to be his own memory of his other life. Now...he watched Lena disappear into that world.

****

Angelina watched from across the street as the two men handed Richard's mother the letter. She didn't need to see the letter to know what it said. Neither did Richard's mother, who fell to her knees as she screamed a piercing, blood-curdling scream. The pain heard in the woman's cry, as well as the horror on her face, equaled Angelina's own heartache, now that she knew. Richard was gone; he'd never return.

Lena roused with a jolt. "You left Angelina," she declared with a grim voice full of grief.

"I did. I'm sorry."

Surprised that Rick admitted this so quickly, Lena could only stare at him.

"What do you remember, Lena?"

"No. I don't remember anything. I saw you with her, it was just...a dream or something. My great-great grandmother...and you?"

"Your great-great grand...no, Lena...*you* were Angelina."

"No. I don't believe it. Why? How would I anyway...how would I come back as my own...no, it just doesn't make sense. That just doesn't happen," Lena said, frightened.

"Who says it doesn't happen?" Rick sounded a trifle annoyed. "From what I've read, souls tend to travel together. So people you've spent time with in one life, tend to find you... in the next."

Lena stood, still unable to grasp the concept of reincarnation. Her headache was coming back. "No, I don't believe any of this." She stormed over to the recliner and sat.

"Why is it that you can believe I was Richard, but not that you were Angelina?" Agitated, Rick stood and paced the room.

Lena mocked a chuckle. "That's another thing, people who are born again come back with the same names? That's crazy." She felt bad though, because Rick looked hurt.

"No, Lena. My name is Patrick. When I slowly began to remember who I was, I started calling myself Rick. It suited me better. And helped me get through...my revelation. I chose my new name. As for you, it's normal to be named after one of your ancestors."

This was just all too much. Now she wanted Rick to leave and forget they ever had this conversation. Why it bothered her to think she could have been Angelina, she had no clue, but it bothered her nonetheless. Her sudden anger toward Rick was irrational too, yet here she was, mad as hell.

"Look, Rick, I'm tired now. I ...just...let yourself out, stay on the couch, I really don't care." She raced to her room and slammed the door, unable to understand what got her so upset. She couldn't deal with it now, not when she had this unwanted pregnancy to deal with.

As soon as her head hit her pillow, she cried. It wasn't like her to get this emotional and the last person she wanted to hurt was Rick. He just made her...furious...and helpless against the circumstances in her life. Though her hostility had come from situations with Vince, she took the easy route and directed it toward Rick. He didn't scare her in the way that Vince did, so it felt safe to do so.

Exhausted and defeated, Lena's tears helped lull her to sleep. However, sometime during the night, she saw Angelina being beaten by that Agnes woman. When Angelina writhed in pain, Lena's own screaming startled her awake. The first thing she saw when she opened her eyes? Rick...seated on her bed, already positioned to take her in his arms.

"Shh," he whispered, wrapping his arms around her. "It's okay, you're awake now. It was only a dream."

It took Lena a moment to compose herself. "Rick." *He hadn't left.* "Why are you still here?" She asked between breaths, still tugging for air after her nightmare.

"Lena, nevermind that. Are you all right? What did you see?"

The tender tone of his voice turned her tumultuous temper to mush.

"Lena, tell me about your dream." His voice, soft and reassuring, made it hard to still be mad at him.

Bringing her knees up to her chest in her ever-favorite seated position, she shook her head. "I saw her again," Lena whispered, her voice so low, she barely heard it herself.

"Angelina?"

"Yes."

Rick's eyes focused on Lena's, but he didn't say a word. Instead, he appeared to be trying to speak to her on a deeper level. Oddly enough, Lena thought she could hear him, if hearing silent words made any sense. She could *feel* his words. Their eyes continued to dive into each other's, until an electric collision of their souls transported them both back to 1917. A surreal moment, where Lena, apart from her current physical self, was standing next to her great-great grandmother, as a young girl. And with the young Angelina, was the boy who broke her heart by going off to war. It was the day they'd said their goodbyes. Lena remembered it from her dream. The one where they'd exchanged the broken locket so each would have a photo of the other. It played out exactly like her dream, only this time, Rick was in the picture, standing next to Richard.

As if lightning had struck, Lena was thrown back into her own time, back into her room. Her heart pounding, breaths quick, she jumped off the bed and panicked, pacing the floor in quick strides. "Ohmigod, ohmigod, ohmigod."

"Lena," Rick stopped her mid-stride, placing his hands on her shoulders.

"Ohmigod, ohmigod..."

"Lena, stop," he yelled. "It's okay."

"Oh my...what just happened?" Her breaths even more rapid, Lena needed to scream and escape herself for the moment. The urge to run took over, and so, she did. Tearing out of the room, down the stairs, and out her front door, she ran out into the dark six a.m. dawn, to who knows where. She felt his steps behind her, but she didn't care. Her feet picked up speed trying to run from her own thoughts...trying to outrun the craziness that had become her life.

His footsteps were still behind her, but he hadn't called out to her. Hadn't tried to stop her. She continued on until she could no longer run at all. Lena dropped to the ground outside the old brick public school she attended in her youth.

"Lena, get up," Rick quietly commanded, while pulling her up by her hands. "It's not good for you to sit when you're so out of breath. C'mon, let's walk it off." Draping his arm around her shoulders, he led them behind the school. Once Lena's breathing returned to normal, Rick brought her to a set of bleachers that overlooked the baseball field.

Lena sat there listening to the sound of her chest expanding and compressing with each breath. Several minutes ticked by before either one of them spoke, but Lena was surprised, and impressed, that Rick would let her vent off steam like that without adding comment or judgment. She'd have to remember that the next time she started to build irrational hostility toward him.

"Thank you," she finally blurted.

"For what?" His genuine uncertainty surprised her.

"For being here, for staying...for not stopping me."

"Now why would I do that? It was scary...what we...experienced... in your bedroom. I was frightened the first time it happened to me, too."

"The first time? You mean...that's happened to you before?"

His quiet titter melted more of the ice that had recently formed over her heart.

"Yes, it's happened to me before; the first time, when I was twelve."

"Twelve? What did you do?" *Run off like a fool, like her?*

"I didn't do anything...at first. Eventually, though, I thought I was going crazy. My mom wanted to put me in a hospital at one point...that's when I ran away."

"You ran away from home?"

"Not for long. I actually met up with someone who proved I *wasn't* crazy."

"Who?"

"Andrew." Rick paused. "He was my younger brother...back then."

"Andrew can remember his past life, too?" She said, amazed.

Again, Rick's nervous laughter created a warm sensation beneath her chest.

"No. Andrew was Andrew in *my* past life. He is still in the same...life...though, I expect, not for long…" He trailed off.

Lena took a moment to think about that. "So, Andrew, as Andrew, was Richard's younger brother?"

"Yes."

"How do you know for sure?"

"Well for one, he owns the building we used to live in. Plus, his memories of Richard matched mine. He was only four when Richard left, but there were things...he remembered. And...he had some actual material things from my past."

"Really? Like what?" Impressed, Lena felt her eyes bug out of her head as she leaned forward to find out what one could actually keep from another lifetime.

"Well, pictures, my, well, Richard's mother's China and some of her jewelry that I can remember her wearing. Other things...anyway, even though there's this tremendous age difference now, he kind of became my...brother...all over again.

We've gotten close over the years. I'm going to miss him." Tears pooled over Rick's eyes, but he blinked them away.

"Rick? How is this all possible? I mean, aside from reincarnation, which I'm still finding hard to believe, how did we...hop into the past?" It took all her will, but she was trying hard to open her mind.

"Well, I've read about Astral Travel or...Astral Projection. I'm not sure if that's what it is when it happens on its own, but I've actually learned to travel to the past on demand...but in your bedroom, I'm not that sure." Rick started squirming on the bench. "I felt an intense...connection, I guess, when we were...staring into each other's eyes...I don't know if you felt it, but it was like we were suddenly plugged in to some electrical charge or something."

"Yeah, I did feel that. I don't know, it's just so...crazy."

"Mmm. It is." He fidgeted again, alerting Lena to his unease.

"Oh, Rick, I wish I could just...shut down, disappear, until this all goes away and, like, wake up when it's all over."

The soft tickle of Rick's fingers caressing her back gave Lena both comfort and butterflies. If only she could be on a regular date...where only one life existed in her world...and no baby existed inside her.

"What is it specifically? The pregnancy or Richard and Angelina...or both?" Though she felt his compassion, she could tell he really wanted her to embrace their past history.

But she wouldn't lie to him. "Both."

His disappointment unmistakable, he smiled politely and pulled her close to his side anyway. "I will help you get through all of it. I promise."

Chapter Thirty-Three

Though Rick returned to work later that day, his thoughts were only on Lena and her consuming turmoil. He should have somehow switched the subject when Lena brought up Richard. Overwhelmed with a new pregnancy to adjust to, Lena did not need to be burdened with a widely-controversial concept. Rick kicked himself for delving further into the subject of reincarnation with her. Right now her priority needed to be her baby, and Rick would keep any subject of their past lives in check. If Lena broached the topic, he would digress, so that her mind could be clear to focus on her immediate future.

Since Lena wasn't in work, he figured it'd be a good time to talk with Pete, the cable company's Director of Studio Operations. It was time Lena got a taste of realizing one of her goals. "Hey Pete, it's Rick," he said when Pete answered his phone.

"Hey Rick, how ya been?"

"Good. How 'bout you?"

"Not bad. What's up?"

"I was just wondering, ya got any positions open over there?"

Pete laughed, "Why, y'thinking ya had enough of managing a buncha techs?"

"Yeah." Rick laughed along with him, but only to keep the tone of the conversation light. "No, seriously, is anything open there?"

"Whatchya have in mind? I am losing one of my camera techs next month. She's enlisted herself in the Navy."

"Wow, cool," Rick thought, thinking how different things are now than when he was in the armed forces almost a hundred years ago. "A camera tech position is exactly what I'm looking for."

Pete let out a cynical chuckle this time. "You lost me, Rick. What do you want with a camera tech position?"

"Well," a more serious Rick began.."You know Dan's new girl, Lena?"

"Yeah, the PR rep?"

"Right, well, her degree is in television. She likes it here, but PR's not really her thing. I mean, she's good at it, and Dan'll have my head if he knows I'm doing this, but...her heart's in production."

"And what's in it for you?" The implications in Pete's tone were unmistakable. How could Rick get around having his feelings found out?

"She's a friend, Pete, that's all...and I'd like to see her happy."

"Mmmm, a friend, huh?"

"Yeah, Pete."

"Right."

"Whaddya say, can she go for it?"

"Yeah, of course. Have her give me her resume. We'd have to go through proper channels, but if she wants it, I'll see what she can do."

"Great. Thanks."

"No problem, just have her talk to Dan before she does anything."

"Right, thanks again."

"See ya."

After the conversation ended, Rick spent most of the rest of the afternoon wondering how Lena'd take the fact that he pulled some strings for her. A timid girl a few months ago, he noticed lately a more feisty version of the girl he fell in love with. He'd hate for her to take his actions as an insult, but he would have to take that chance. She needed to know that she didn't have to toss her dreams aside just because she thought it was too late. One lifetime for that mistake was one too many.

This time, Rick would see to it that Lena did not settle. When Richard died, before his soul went to wherever it went, he recalled watching

Angie from the sidelines. He watched her mother beat her senseless and he watched her run into the arms of that loathsome Timothy, who reminded Rick so much of Vince. Deceased, Richard could not help Angie realize a better life. But Rick certainly could come to Lena's rescue now. Would she appreciate his butting into her life? Though they shared the same soul, Lena was different than Angie...more evolved.

The longer he thought about it, the more he realized she'd probably take offense. For a man a few years away from forty, he sure felt like a love-struck teenager playing these little games. He had to call Pete. The receiver shook in his hand while it rang on the other end; he couldn't understand his own nervous emotions. "Hey, Pete, Rick again." He sighed.

"Hey guy, what's up?"

Betraying his now racing heart, he feigned laughter. "Um, would you mind calling Lena yourself and, um, asking her to apply for the position? I'm, um, thinking she may not like...my involvement too much."

"Friends, huh? Yeah, I believe that...how 'bout I call Dan first and tell him I heard about his new employee's degree and wanted to...enlist her myself? This way, I won't be stepping on anyone's toes."

"Good idea. I owe you one."

"Nah, what are friends for?"

The racing stopped. Calmness overcame Rick. Thank goodness. When he noticed time approaching four o'clock, he hustled to get some paperwork done, not wanting to fall too far behind. After work, he called Lena before heading home to Sparta. He desperately needed that shower. Fortunately, he'd had a spare shirt in his Jeep, but a good wash was essential. Lena would be having dinner with her parents and most likely, spending the night, so Rick had been instructed, kindly, to not bother coming down. *'Don't call me, I'll call you,'* implied.

From the center of his heart, he knew Lena would need time alone…knew she would retreat from Rick's presence, but disappointment still knocked the wind out of him. As much as he wanted Lena to need him, he had become much too obsessed with her well-being. His love, so deep and intense, he could no longer see beyond what mattered to her. Yes, it struck like a punch in the gut when she implied she would rather not see him, but her needs would always come first. If he could go back to 1917 and change things, he would take Angie and desert the country; escape America somehow, just to keep her near him. Hindsight meant nothing now. Angelina had already suffered that lifetime, because Richard had deserted her. In this lifetime, Rick would do whatever it took to stop her suffering. Her soul could not take much more. If staying away was what she needed, then Rick would stay away.

****

After a full week off from work, Lena reluctantly returned, ready to focus on something other than her problems but not ready to see Rick. She knew she should have never brushed him off the way she had, but seeing him prompted memories of their supernatural step back in time. Too freaky to accept, Lena would rather repress the memory. Her daily nausea helped her to do so, since most days, her churning stomach stopped her from thinking most anything else. Though mentally she needed to return to a regular work schedule, she hoped, physically, she could handle it.

The morning naturally flew by. Piles of paperwork kept her busy enough to skip lunch, and by mid-afternoon, she had finally made a dent when her in-house phone line lit up. "Hello, this is Lena."

"Lena Giordano?" Said a man's voice she didn't recognize.

"Yes. May I help you?"

"This is Pete Taylor, from Studio Ops."

"Oh, hi, what can I do for you?"

"Well, I hear you studied television production."

"Yes, I did. Why?" Confusion started to set in for Lena. What did this man want?

"Well, we have a camera tech position opening soon, would you like to apply?"

An unfamiliar thrill stirred deep in the center of her stomach. "Oh. Yes." She paused, not sure of protocol. "I would have to talk with Dan first, but yes, I'd love to. I can send you my resume." The rousing enthusiasm built so quickly that Lena, simultaneously, feared the crashing of another hope.

"Great. Send it inter-office mail, then make sure to see Human Resources. It won't be posted until tomorrow, though."

"Thank you so much." A grateful Lena hung up.

As soon as finishing the conversation, Lena ran to the ladies' room to throw up. Splashing water on her face afterwards, she wondered how she could make this work. It would be a dream come true to get behind a studio camera; God knew how hard she worked in college. But with a new baby on the way, would it be impossible? Jules would help, her mother had already assured her of that. Lena smiled in spite of herself, allowing the burning desire in the hollow of her stomach to stay ignited. If all went well, she could actually be working in a real television studio, just like she'd always imagined.

Chapter Thirty-Four

The months went by in a flash. By October, Lena had settled comfortably into her new position as Camera Operations Technician. Her twenty-sixth birthday passed with a spaghetti and meatball dinner and pumpkin pie, compliments of Jules. Lena had successfully repressed any thoughts of Richard and Angelina, but in order to do that, she sadly avoided Rick, ignoring his phone calls and knocks on the door. He knew better than to call the police again, but it made her melancholy, nonetheless, to hurt him. Lena had to look out for herself, though, and so she continued to shun the one man she knew who really loved her.

Instead of concentrating on missing Rick, Lena threw her whole heart into her new job. Her boss Pete had been so impressed with Lena's work, that he'd promoted her from third camera person to first camera person within three months. Now he'd been talking about having her direct a cable program or two. Finally, Lena felt a sense of accomplishment. With one aspect of her life falling into place, she had hope for other facets to tumble peacefully into position.

Today had been a quiet day, not much different than other Saturdays, but today Lena was racked with guilt. It was October twentieth, the day she would have married Vince Battaglia. The day she would have made the biggest mistake of her life. Never mind she'd already misconstrued her feelings toward Vince, thinking all he needed was love and acceptance to be a nicer person. In the end, her own empathy and compassion had taken her down the wrong path. Fortunately, by realizing her own self-worth, she'd found a new path, a brighter path. And though she'd secretly wished Rick were walking along with her, she knew it best to leave that relationship alone. Yes, having the courage to walk away from an abusive man helped her self-esteem, but Lena still felt too unstable to begin something new. Especially with a new baby coming in a few months, Lena needed to give all she had to the new love in her life. Her baby.

As the fetus inside of her grew, so did the love for her child, grow within her heart. Gone was the nagging reminder of her baby's conception. Present was the unconditional adoration for the miracle who would soon become a living and breathing human being. A child, who she would offer her never-ending love and protection. Amazed at her heart's transformation toward her little one, she was extremely grateful for it, as well.

A sudden crash tore Lena from her musing. Seconds later, what sounded like the shattering of glass and the tumbling of wood came from the other room. Her instincts were to run and see what was happening, but by the time she left her bedroom, she heard a thundering wrap on the door, before it crashed down in front of her...Vince, on the other side.

Now, Lena knew she needed to run, but she couldn't get by him to get down the stairs, so she bounded for the window in her bedroom. Jammed shut. Instead, heading for the corner, she cowered, fearful of Vince in this drunken state. She needed to calm him. "Vince, it's okay." Trembling and lightheaded, she continued anyway, "I'm here...for you," she said, teeth chattering.

"You whore." Vince vaulted over the bed, not bothering to walk around it, but rather heading right toward Lena.

With her eyes closed, Lena could still feel him in front of her. His hands, cold and clammy on her wrist, she smelled the foul stench of alcohol on his breath. "Vince, no."

He grabbed the back of her collar, the waist of her pants, and lifting her above the floor, he threw her across the room. Landing on the floor aside her bed, she hit the nightstand, its corner meeting the edge of her eye. Lena pushed herself off the floor with her hands, came to her feet, and bolted toward the door. Vince caught her in the doorway and tossed her again into the living room coffee table. Lena's forehead whacked it hard, causing a blackened room.

"You're a friggin' bitch," he exclaimed, while Lena lay, near unconscious, on the floor. "Get up, witch." He kicked her in her side.

"Vince, stop," she squeaked, trying to gather the strength to get off the floor. "The baby, please."

"The baby? You mean that bastard? He ain't mine and you know it." Vince pushed her back down onto the coffee table.

This time Lena got to her feet quickly, jockeying herself around Vince and making it to the door leading to the stairwell.

"Who the hell were you sleeping with while..."

But Lena couldn't hear the rest of his drunken rant while running for the stairs. When she took the first step down, at once, the sole of his boot on her lower back registered in her mind, before time stood still and she was suspended in mid-air. Toppling like a ragdoll down the stairs, the bottom floor seemed so far away. In an instant, everything was gone.

****

Rick sat up straight in his chair. Something was wrong. He knew it. He felt it.

Lena.

Leaving no time to stop and think, he grabbed his keys and his cell and jumped on his bike. The motorcycle would be faster. Before turning on the ignition, Rick phoned Lena, realizing he probably wouldn't get an answer. Correct in his assumption, he started the bike and flew. Understanding that he needed to alert someone, he pulled to the side of the road and called Frank. If he wasn't at the liquor store, certainly someone would answer. After calling information, he got Frank on the phone. "Frank, I'm a friend of Lena's. My name is Rick. I think your daughter's in trouble." The words tumbled out in a rush.

"Who is this, and what kind of joke are you playing?"

"It's not a joke, sir. It's just a hunch. Could you humor me and please just check on her? Please," Rick pleaded.

Silence met him on the other end.

"Mr. Giordano, I'm going by instinct here, but I'm a close friend of Lena's, and I really think she's in trouble. I wouldn't kid you about this."

Still silence, then a dial-tone. *Damn.*

Rick pulled back onto the road, satisfied. Assured by the amount of love Frank had for his daughter that he wouldn't ignore Rick's pleading request.

Chapter Thirty-Five

Rick's heart pounded to the beat of the flashing of the blue and red neon lights set atop the cop car that sat in front of Lena's apartment complex. Barely putting his bike in park, he jumped off, not bothering with the kickstand, and ran for Lena. On the porch, Lena lay prostrate, encumbered in a brace on a stretcher.

"Lena," Rick called out in vain. She wouldn't respond to his call.

She couldn't. She lay there still, unable to move.

"Frank?" The short, stocky man turned to the man calling his name. "I'm Rick. The one who phoned..."

"What the hell do you know about this?" Frank, though half a foot shorter, grabbed Rick by the collar.

Hands up in defense, Rick assured, "Not a thing. It was intuition, I get it a lot."

Frank's furrowed brow alerted Rick to the man's suspicions, but Rick's collar was released, and Frank went back to his daughter.

"Sir," the paramedic informed Frank. "We'll be bringing her to Saint Joe's in Paterson. There's a trauma center there. Would you like to come with us in the ambulance, or meet us there?"

For some reason, Frank looked at Rick.

"You go with her," Rick directed. "I'll follow. I can call her mother." Calling his wife was an obvious oversight during the commotion, Rick gathered. "I know the house, if she's home, I'll go over and get her. I can bring her to the ER," Rick offered.

"No. Lena's never mentioned you," Frank answered. "I'll call her now. Um..."

An officer approached. "Frank, I'll give Jules a visit. If one of your sons isn't there to give her a ride, I'll do it."

"Thanks, Scott. Okay, good." Frank left with the ambulance.

Scott the officer sauntered over to Rick. "Rick, is it?"

"Yes." Rick held out his hand in greeting, but Scott disregarded it. "Rick Murphy."

"You're the one who called Mr. Giordano?"

"Yes." Knowing where this was going, Rick volunteered his services. "Would you like me to give you a statement?"

Officer Scott appeared a bit taken back, clearly surprised by Rick's offer. "Yes, I would. However, I'd like to inform Mrs. Giordano, right now. Would you mind meeting me at the station?"

Yes, I'd mind, I need to see Lena. "No, not at all." Rick comprehended his predicament; he needed to cooperate fully, so as not to give anyone the wrong impression.

Inside the small Haledon police department, Officer Nagel instructed Rick to jot down his statement while waiting for Officer Scott.

"Mr. Murphy, Officer Brannigan asked that you sit tight; he's on his way back now." Officer Nagel walked out of the room, but not before leaving Rick with a look of repugnance. Rick knew why. *Guilty until proven innocent.* But it mattered little to Rick. If the paramedics got there in time to save Lena's life, then let them think Rick guilty. He just wished he knew what actually happened.

Scott barreled in a few moments later with the same expression of disgust that his comrade had shown earlier. Pulling out the chair and spinning it around, Scott straddled the chair. "Tell me, Mr.," he looked down at the paper Rick wrote on, "Murphy, how'd you just happen to know that our victim was lying at the bottom of a stairwell?"

Rick flinched; he hadn't known that's where they'd found Lena. "I didn't know where she was or how hurt she was, I only had a feeling that she was in troub..."

"You had a feeling?" The officer mocked.

"Yes. I have...a strong bond with Lena and...it was intuition, at best."

"It was intuition," Scott parroted.

Rick could not help but feel deflated. "Yes, sir, intuition." Rick sighed in defeat.

"Then you called her father, who has never heard of you, though you say you have a strong bond with his daughter."

"Yes, I do." Trying to contain himself, Rick took a few deep breaths, hoping to avoid an outburst.

"Mr. Murphy, this sounds like hogwash to me. What do you know? Did you beat Miss Giordano and push her down the stairs?"

"No. I did not."

"You're lying."

"No, I am not."

"You are," Scott exclaimed, while at the same time, slamming his fist on the table.

"No, Sir." Keeping his composure was becoming a challenge. "I assure you, I am not lying. I had a hunch that Lena was in danger, and I needed to alert someone, just in case. I live too far away to have checked on her myself."

"Yet…here you are."

This officer will be the death of Rick yet. Maintaining the dignity he so diligently tried to uphold, Rick responded slowly. "I got on my bike as soon as I realized, but it took me forty-five minutes to get here. It could have been too late."

"Sir, you're either crazy or guilty. My guess is, you're both."

"Really?" Rick was floored. How was he going to get through, to this ignorant officer, his innocence? "I don't know what else you want me to say, sir. I don't even know what happened. Until you just mentioned it, I had no idea she was even found at the bottom," sudden nausea caused Rick to pause at the words, "of the stairwell."

"You live in Sparta, it says here."

"Yes, sir."

"Don't go leaving the state. Now get outta here."

Rick left and headed for the hospital, realizing that he probably wouldn't be welcomed there either. Instead, he phoned Betty, filled her in on what had transpired, and asked if she could help him find out how Lena was doing.

Betty met Rick at the hospital and escorted him in.

"I appreciate your coming so quickly, Betty. I know how this must look to her family, but truly, it was just a hunch...that I happened to be right about."

Betty patted Rick's shoulder. "So they found her at the bottom of her stairwell, beaten and unconscious?"

"Yup. It had to be that no-good ex-fiancé of hers."

"*Ex*-fiancé? I hadn't realized they'd broken up."

"Really?" Rick was surprised Betty hadn't heard about it.

"Well, remember, I haven't seen her much since she'd gotten that studio job. She keeps in touch with Lindsey still, I think, but, well, I hadn't heard," Betty confessed.

"Oh," responded a sullen Rick.

"Hi there." Betty approached the receptionist in the emergency room. "We're friends of Lena Giordano."

"Okay." The woman took a minute to refer to her computer. "Actually, they're admitting her into Intensive Care right now. It'll be a while, but you'll have to go to the main entrance to see her."

"Great, thank you," Betty responded and turning to leave, they saw Frank Giordano hurrying out the door.

"Mr. Giordano?" It was crucial that Rick confront him, though he knew he'd be met with a stone expression and that familiar look of repulsion. "Is she all right?"

Facing Rick square in the face, Frank opened his mouth. "I'd like to know one thing. If you weren't the one who did this, how did you know to call me?" Frank put his hand up, halting Rick's response. "And I don't believe that you just had a hunch."

"But I did, sir. Your daughter may never have mentioned me, but we are good friends and there is a bond between us...I...just..." Rick trailed off, his explanation falling on deaf ears.

Frank turned to Betty, maybe for affirmation, maybe not, but Betty replied, "Mr. Giordano, I'm also a friend of Lena's and a co-worker. We both are. Rick would not lie...and they are very good friends."

A guttural sigh came from Frank, an apparent sign of exasperation of the whole ordeal. "She's in a coma. They're admitting her into ICU now, you might as well follow me over. We're just waiting."

In the waiting room, a middle-aged woman, a young woman about twenty-something, and four young men, ranging in age from mid-teens to mid-twenties, were quietly conversing. Dried tears evident in their eyes and on their cheeks. Frank broke the silent chatter. "This is my family. Family, these are Lena's friends."

The polite, sullen family all stood to greet the newcomers.

"Mrs. Giordano," Rick started. "I'm so sorry to meet you under these circumstances. I'm Rick Murphy." He held out his hand in greeting. "A co-worker and friend of Lena's."

"Hello," the somber woman replied, shaking Rick's hand.

"I'm Betty, also a co-worker and friend of your daughter." The two women also greeted each other with a handshake.

"Hello, I'm sorry." Jules ran off, tissue to her eyes, toward the rest room.

Francis, Katrina, Antonio, Nicholas and Christopher all greeted Betty and Rick, then dispersed back to their seats, with the exception of Katrina, who remained standing near Rick. Betty seemed to have read something on Katrina's face, because she suddenly left to get herself a cup of coffee.

"Lena's mentioned you to me."

Rick must have appeared as shocked as he felt, because Katrina chuckled a little.

"She has?"

"Yes. Just once. And only in passing, but...the way her eyes lit up when she said she was going to see a co-worker," Katrina made air quotes around the word co-worker, "perform at The Tavern, I just knew she'd call off her engagement."

Gratitude filled every ounce of him. He was so happy and relieved to hear that. "You did, huh?"

"Yup. I know my sister...better than I think she knows herself."

"Hmmm. How do you know she was talking about me?" He had to be sure.

Katrina found this amusing as well. "I asked who her co-worker was. She said, 'some guy named Rick Murphy.'

"Yeah, that'd be me."

"Mm-hmm." Katrina smiled. "It's nice to meet you, Rick Murphy, and whatever you did to get her away from Vince, thank you."

"Mmm, I didn't get her away fast enough."

"You mean before she got pregnant? Wait a minute...It's not yours is it?"

"No, no, no, not at all, your sister and I haven't...no, never. But, yes, I mean I wish she got away before the pregnancy and, um, before...tonight."

"Wait. You think Vince did this?"

"Well, what do you all think?"

"My dad thought you did it, but we just assumed someone broke in. Why would you think Vince would do something like this?"

Rick did not want to betray Lena's trust, but her family needed to know. "Katrina, aside from this being the day they were supposed to get married, he is brutal to her. Maybe he's good at hiding it, but..." He wasn't sure he wanted to divulge this information, but he knew he should. "He rapes her, he beats her, he torments her."

Katrina was clearly shocked. Speechless.

"I'm sorry to tell you that."

Katrina interrupted. "We already knew about his forcing himself on her, but...I don't think anyone knew he was beating her." Katrina looked crestfallen. "We only thought the forcing was, well, just a boyfriend/girlfriend thing, I don't think we realized he had been raping her repeatedly. I mean, my dad was furious as hell, but we really thought it had just been that one time. Oh my god."

The darkness that fell across his heart, hearing it all out loud, was too much to bear. "I'm sorry, Katrina, I need to leave for a minute." Rick ran out of the room, down the hall, down the elevator, and out of the hospital. He had never said those things out loud, nor did he ever hear them said. He ran to the nearest bush and vomited.

Chapter Thirty-Six

Over the next few days, Rick had gotten pretty close to the Giordano family. They accepted him as Lena's friend, while appreciating his honesty about Lena's relationship with Vince and the possibility that Vince could have been the one to have put Lena in this position. Once the Haledon Police were informed, the Battaglias were notified and Vince, questioned. Though the Battaglias tried to claim his innocence, and though advised not to speak without his lawyer present, Vince eventually cracked under the pressure of the policemen's questioning. Frank informed Rick and the rest of the Giordanos that, though Mr. Battaglia had tried to protect his son, Vince went crazy, admitting everything. The Haledon PD had Vince in a holding cell temporarily, but they were trying to get him admitted into a psychiatric ward until his arraignment.

Meanwhile, Lena remained comatose in Intensive Care while Rick continually sat by her side. Jules stayed much of the time as well, leaving only to go home and sleep in her own bed.

"Rick, sweetie." Jules tapped the dozing man on his arm. "Why don't you go home and get some sleep? You've been here four straight days. Go. Take a shower, get some rest."

"No. I'm fine, Mrs. G. As long as the nurses aren't kicking me out, I'm staying."

Jules just stared at him.

"What?" Rick asked.

"Why hadn't Lena mentioned you?"

"I imagine...she was embarrassed about having feelings for me, while only recently breaking up with her fiancé. I'm sure her family's opinion of her came into play."

"Mmm. Well, we only always wanted what was best for her. I wish she knew that."

"I think, Mrs. Giordano, she never really knew what was best for herself."

"Mmm."

Rick watched tears pool in Lena's mother's eyes. "Y'know." He stood to meet her eye to eye, "Lena will be all right. I feel it."

Jules smiled. "One of your hunches?"

"Yeah. One of my hunches."

"I'll see you in the morning, Rick. Bring you coffee?"

"Sure. Thanks."

Rick sure hoped this hunch was correct. It wasn't a strong one, but it rippled through him like a gentle wave hitting the shore. He knelt by her bed and prayed...for what seemed like hours. While he was doing so, Lena's hand moved beneath his arm, the warm tickle alerting his senses. His head jerked up. "Lena?"

Her eyes flickered.

"Nurse, Nur..." But the nurse had already been notified by the monitor that was connected to the nurses' station, because she'd entered the room before he'd finished calling her. "She just..." Rick was dumbstruck.

The nurse pushed a few buttons on the monitor and checked her pulse. "Her heart rate is picking up."

Lena's eyes flickered again. This time, her eyelids actually opened half way. Rick ran to the other side and grabbed her hand. "Lena. Oh Lena, I'm right here." He kissed her hand, her forehead, her arm, relishing her warm skin beneath his lips.

"Mr. Murphy," the nurse intoned. "Let me finish, please."

"Oh, yeah, sure. Can I hold her hand?" A stirred Rick asked with unrestrained joy.

"Yes."

The light glistening off Lena's dark brown eyes was an answered prayer. She was awake. "Lena. You're awake," Rick announced.

Lena only blinked.

He felt the blood drain from his face.

"Give her time," the nurse sympathized.

"She can't talk?" His bubble burst.

"I'm sure she can." The nurse kept her eyes on Lena. "Give her time." She picked up her phone. "This is Liz, call Doctor Olsen to Room 18. She's up."

"Mr. Murphy, why don't you give us a few minutes, you can call her family."

"Sure." His heart sunk heavily in his chest. *What if she never returned back to normal? What if her brain was damaged?*

The phone picked up on the first ring. "Hello?" Jules asked nervously.

"She's up..." Unable to finish his sentence, because Jules immediately hung up, Rick was hoping to at least fill her in, so as not to get her hopes too far up. Like his did.

After about forty minutes, Doctor Olsen came out into the waiting area, where Rick, Jules, and Frank were pacing the room. "You can see her now. I just need to tell you, she's not one hundred percent yet. She's confused as to what year it is. A little disoriented, as well. But…she is awake and maybe, by seeing you, you'll trigger an awareness."

The four of them silently approached Lena's room. Rick stood in the background to allow Lena's parents to reacquaint with their daughter. He stayed behind the curtain, uncertain of Lena's reaction to seeing him.

"Lena, sweetie," Rick heard Jules cry.

"Hey, Lena," Frank uttered quietly.

"Hi," Lena breathed, causing a slight tear in Rick's heart. His Lena sounded so weak and fragile. *But at least she was speaking.*

"Lena." Now Rick heard the Doctor speak up. "Do you know who these two people are?"

"Yeeess." Her answer, still soft, seemed unsure. "Mmmma."

"That's right, Lena," Doctor Olson responded. "Your mother. Do you recognize the man?"

"Ddddaaaddd."

"Yes, your father. Very good."

"She can't speak?" Jules asked.

"Yes," Doc Olson replied. "It'll just take her a while to remember how. She wasn't in a coma long, but her body was still only functioning at bare minimum. It'll take her a little bit to readjust."

"Oh. You mentioned she's confused about the year?" Frank asked.

"Lena, tell me what year it is."

"Niiiinneteeen ssssev sssseventteeenn."

Rick felt all his energy leave his body. He lost his balance, knocking into the table and causing a ruckus behind the curtain.

"Oh, Rick," Frank called out, pulling the curtain back. "What are you doing back there? C'mon, come see her, you've been with her all this time."

Rick moved at a slow pace toward Lena. "Hello, Lena," he said timidly.

Her smile quickly spread across her face, almost reaching from ear to ear. "Rrriiichaaard. Yoooou caaame baaaackk."

His heavy heart smarted as he realized who she thought he was. "Hey there." Rick bent down and kissed her forehead. "How ya feel, sweetheart?"

"Haapppy yooour baaaackk fffrrromm wwwaaar."

The walls began caving in on Rick as he tried to figure out how to explain things to Lena's parents. More importantly, how would he untangle Lena's raveled mind?

"War?" Frank questioned the doctor. "I don't understand, why does she think it's nineteen seventeen and Rick is back from the war?"

"I'm not sure, Mr. Giordano. It is common that a person just out of a coma is disoriented about time. But almost a hundred years off is, unfortunately, not commonplace. She could have been dreaming while comatose. She should regain her full memory soon, though."

Rick's heart bled, watching her face crumple in confusion. "Rrrrichhaard? Wwwhaat isss wrrrongg?" Lena struggled with her question.

Words were not finding their way... but tears were. Both Rick and Jules could not contain their own emotions, while Frank remained composed.

"Rick, is that your full name? Richard?" Mr. Giordano asked.

Still speechless, Rick could only shake his head.

"Then who does Lena think you are?" Frank again questioned him.

Rick knew it was too soon to mention reincarnation, Frank just got over thinking Rick was crazy for having an intuition about Lena's fall. What would her parents think about his past life experiences? Lena hadn't even believed it herself. Rick was between a rock and a hard place, with no idea how to get out. In the end, he just shrugged his shoulders in response to Frank's inquiry, pleading ignorance instead.

The beeping on the heart monitor picked up pace. Hurrying into the room, the nurse ran to Lena's side and checked her vitals. After a few moments, she turned an austere eye on the visitors. "Lena's distressed right now, you need to allow her to rest. She will not heal effectively if she is disturbed." The nurse softened her tone. "Please, go get yourselves something to eat, a cup of coffee, something. Come back in a couple hours. She's scheduled for an MRI at 11. Come back after that."

After all of them gave Lena a kiss on the forehead, they left the room. Jules and Frank went for coffee; Rick opted for the waiting area to think. Not ten minutes later, Lena's nurse came in to see Rick. "Mr. Murphy, Lena is asking for you and...well, she's insisting she see you."

"Oh." Rick stood, eager to see her. "Sure."

"Hey, Leen," he greeted her, pasting a smile on his face, even though it killed him to see her this way.

"Lleeenna? Sssincce whennn?" Lena struggled again with her words.

"Sorry...Angie. How's your head?"

"Hurrtss."

Rick turned his attention to the nurse. "Does she know what this is?" He asked, pointing to the television hanging from the wall. "She must be confused," he whispered.

The nurse called Rick to the side of the room. "Yes, we asked her. It seems Lena is familiar with some things, but like I said, she's a bit disoriented."

"So, she recognized her parents, but not...never mind." Rick wanted to say that she didn't remember him, at least not Patrick Murphy, anyway.

He left the nurse and went back to Lena's side. Her hand reached for his, comforting him with her gentle squeeze. With a tender touch, he stroked her palm with his fingers.

"Could you give us a moment?" Rick looked at the nurse. "I mean, I realize you need to supervise, but will you excuse our conversation?"

With the nurse's nod, Rick took both Lena's hands, even her intravenous encumbered hand. "Sweetie, do you remember the conversation we had about past lives?"

Her wide eyes and blank expression told Rick she didn't.

"Sweetheart, I *was* Richard, but in a past life. You were Angie. We loved each other, but I got drafted into the war and never came back. I was killed. Do you remember that?"

Rick noticed recognition flash through her mind. He saw it in her eyes.

"*Now* I am Rick... Patrick... Patrick Murphy. But... I remember you as Angie. My Angie," he whispered. "Only now... you are Lena," Rick smiled when the corners of her mouth turned up. "Angelina Giordano, not Angelina Mancini."

"My grrreatt-grrrammother," she stated.

"Yes, Leen. *You* were your Nana, in our past life."

Lena reached for her coveted locket, which no longer hung from her neck.

"Yes, Lena, the locket you wear was your Nana's. Mimi's mom. Do you remember that?"

Lena nodded, and a tear crawled down her cheek. Then, another. Before long, tears poured from her eyes, causing a bemused Rick. "What? What is it?"

"I re...rememmmbberr...evvrrythhingg."

"Everything?"

She nodded.

"Agnes?"

All he got was a blank stare.

"Do you remember *this* life?"

Rick was met with another blank stare. He wasn't sure what she remembered...or if she was afraid to admit what she remembered. Rick sensed that she was afraid of what was going on in her mind. He was sure this was all too overwhelming to her right now. Instead, Rick decided silence was best.

But something was going through Lena's mind. Her eyes were wide in shock and she suddenly looked afraid.

"Vvvince."

"Yes, Vince." Rick's blood began to boil. "He did this to you."

Lena nodded and sobbed, again.

The nurse walked up behind Rick and put her hand on his shoulder. "Let her rest now. You've been helpful...and interesting. Let her think about everything right now. You can come back later."

The tip of Lena's nose was cool when he kissed her goodbye. "Sweet dreams, Lena. I'll see you in a little while." His heavy heart held the burden of Lena's troubles, and he wished dearly that he could take her pain away.

Chapter Thirty-Seven

"My baby, my baby," Lena woke in a sweat, screaming from her hospital bed.

"Shh. Honey, it's okay. Your baby is fine," Jules assured her daughter with her words and a comforting hand stroking her stomach. "He's fine. He's healthy, his heart rate is just where it should be."

"Mom?"

"Yes, Dear?"

"What day is it?"

"It's Tuesday, why?"

"I forgot."

"You forgot that it was Tuesday?"

"No, that I was pregnant. Why didn't you remind me?" Lena nearly cried.

"The doctor wanted you to remember on your own," Jules said, softly. "He said it may take a few days, especially since you haven't gotten out of bed or anything to see yourself."

"It's a boy?" Lena whispered, her stomach tingling thinking about it.

"Yes. You're having a baby boy."

"Hmmm...Mom?"

"Yes?"

"Where's Rick?"

"He's downstairs with Dad. You know, that man only left twice since you've been here...and not once while you were in the coma. He really is something. He really cares about you, honey."

"Yeah, I know." A dark hole filled her mind where Rick was concerned; it only added confusion to her already hazy thoughts.

"Sweetie." A cautious Jules seemed to proceed tentatively. "The nurses said you've been having quite...the nightmares. Do you want to talk about them?"

"Um, I don't know...I just..." Lena didn't finish, she only stared into space.

"Were you having nightmares before your accident?

Lena shook her head. "Not like this."

"You've been waking up screaming, they tell me. Nearly hyperventilating. Would you like to talk to someone about them? A therapist or something?"

Yes. No. What could she say? Anyone she told would think she was crazy. For the past several nights, Lena had spent her sleeping hours back in the early twentieth century. She didn't like it. Already accustomed to dreams about Agnes beating the pulp out of Angelina, she now witnessed the beatings of her great-great grandmother by her great-great grandfather, Timothy. At least Lena believed that's who her recent dreams were about. But then Rick's words kept coming back to haunt her. *She was her own great-great grandmother in a previous life.* Could he be right? The thought made her want to puke. She knew he was right. She remembered. But, no, maybe it was the trick of her own mind. Yeah, she'd go with that. "Mom?"

"Yes, sweetheart?"

"How much of Nana's life do you know about?"

"Nana? What brought that on?"

"My dreams. They're about someone named Angelina, but...it's not me."

"Does she look like Nana?"

Lena frowned, "I'm not sure. Mimi only had one old picture of her. Grandma Leanne didn't have any either. I *think* it was her."

"What were they about?"

"She's being abused. All the time. Maybe it's my imagination, but...," not sure how to say it, Lena bit the bullet and proceeded, "I feel like it all happened to me."

"The abuse?"

"Yes." She closed her eyes, fearful her mother would think her crazy.

"Maybe...you're just projecting what Vince has done to you, onto someone else, so...it doesn't seem so...personal."

"Hmmm." Lena thought about that. Her mother had a point.

"I don't know, honey. I'm not a psychiatrist or anything like that, but...it sounds plausible."

"Yeah. You're right. I bet that's all it is." Lena liked her mother's theory, and it definitely made more sense than Rick's reincarnation thing. Her mind was playing tricks, that's all, she thought, more to convince herself than anything.

"Sweetheart, the doctor did not want us to push your thoughts, but...do you remember saying you were in the year nineteen seventeen...and thinking Rick had just come back from the war?"

Yes, Lena remembered, but she didn't want to. It scared her to admit it, because then she'd have to admit that it was possible for reincarnation to exist and that it wasn't just her imagination. That would open the flood gates for even more psychological distress. With a baby on the way, Lena would just not allow any more unwanted situations in her life. "Hmmm," she replied to her mother. "I thought it was the year nineteen seventeen? When?"

Lena watched a deflated Jules frown. "Oh, never mind, sweetie, forget I said anything."

"Okay." Lena faked a laugh, feeling bad for lying to her mother.

Just then Rick walked in.

"Hi there, Rick," a now smiling Jules greeted him. "She's doing much better this morning. Her speech is more fluent; the doctor is happy with her recovery."

"Great, Jules. Hey Leen, you look great," a visibly unsure Rick addressed Lena.

"Thanks," she said half-heartedly.

The rippling sensation of warmth that spread through her when he took her hand and kissed her forehead added more uncertainty to Lena's fragile state. The mocking confusion between her increasing love for Rick and her frequent agitation toward him, lent to her feeling restless and flustered. At times, she'd wished Rick had never entered her life. Then again, that would be a lie; he was all she could think about.

"Well, let me leave you two alone," Jules chimed in. "I'll go get a bite to eat downstairs. Be back in a bit." She kissed her daughter on the cheek and left.

"So," Rick began. "Are you feeling any better?"

"A little." Lena wanted to keep the conversation short, just as she had the past few days. What could she say to him? She'd rather him not be around. If he were out of the picture, her nightmares would certainly dissipate; they'd only gotten so bad since meeting Rick. Before then, she'd only have little spurts that made no sense. Now, they were scary and out of hand. She just wanted the craziness to disappear...and that included Rick.

"Well, I'm sure you'll feel better soon, sweetheart."

"Mmm." Trying not to lead him on any further, Lena averted her eyes, attempting to ignore him...hating herself for doing so.

"Lena, what's up? What's going on?" She heard the tremble in his voice; felt his sadness in her heart.

She fiddled with her blankets, while keeping her eyes down.

"Lena." He lifted her chin gently with his two fingers, effecting eye to eye contact. "What's going on?"

She sighed, unable to contain the pain in her heart.

"Would you like me to...go away?" he asked quietly.

A few tiny nods, all she could muster, she choked back her tears. When she tried to open her mouth to say something, the lump in her throat grew so large she could no longer hold back her tears.

"Why? Can I ask why you want me to leave?" His voice remained barely above a whisper, and Lena had a feeling he was holding back his own tears.

The pain in her chest crushed her heart. She shook her head. "I don't know." She barely heard her own words.

"You don't know?" She could hear his voice loud and clear now. His anger could not be mistaken. "That's it? You don't know?" He waited, probably for her response, which never came. "Well, gee, Lena, that's a fine reason to want me to go away. You don't know," an unquestionably upset Rick, mocked. "Well, now I feel so much better...now that I know the reason that is."

"Rick, I'm sorry," she cried, not wanting to see him so upset.

He sat down beside her, on the edge of the bed. "Lena, I don't understand." Calmer, Rick placed his fingertips on her wrist. "I know you love me. I feel it. I see it. God, Lena, all that we've been through."

"What?" Lena interjected, still teary-eyed. "What have we been through? A couple dates? That's nothing."

"Oh, okay. I get it. You don't believe we had a past together, is that it?"

"Yes," she snipped.

"Well...even so, you do love me. I know you do. I can't be wrong about that."

The tears rolling down Rick's cheeks stabbed at her heart. She hated to hurt him, but what could she do? Scared and pregnant and treading on unknown territory, Lena had no answers. She turned and stared out the window, unable to look at the pain of betrayal in Rick's eyes.

"So that's it then? I leave and walk out of your life forever...and that's okay with you?" His voice trembled.

Lena kept her attention on the stillness of the trees outside the window. She couldn't look at him. Her heart wanted him, but her head was too overwhelmed with all the chaos going on in her life. Her ex-fiancé almost pushed her and her baby to their death. She's supposed to turn around and trust another man after that? Lena was too confused to think. She could not deal with Rick right now.

Rick met her silence with, "I guess it is," then he stormed out of the room...leaving Lena alone with a crushing heart. But she wouldn't let him know that. She couldn't let him know that. It'd only encourage him.

Chapter Thirty-Eight

Though Rick was surrounded by the usual crowd of barflies at The Tavern, he was lonely – his forsaken heart silently screaming for the woman who turned him away. He considered canceling his performance, but music was usually therapeutic for him, and he was hoping tonight would be no exception. But until nine o'clock rolled around, he figured he'd sit at the bar and have a couple whiskey sours to still his disquieted heart.

"Hey there, good-looking," a soft voice said, as a tender hand caressed the back of his neck.

"Gina," an unimpressed Rick replied.

"Where've ya been? We've missed you 'round here," commented The Tavern's head waitress.

"Mmm. Been here and there." He did not want to get into a conversation with her. Sulking was all that was on his mind.

Gina continued to rub the back of his neck, inching her fingers suggestively through his hair. Rick closed his eyes, enjoying the affection, longing for Lena. He did nothing to discourage the touching, so Gina pulled up a stool, practically sitting on his lap. Though Lena was in his heart, he couldn't deny that the touch of a woman felt good. The liquor filled him with that familiar warm sensation, while Gina's fondling fingers aroused other pleasant feelings.

"Wanna meet up after your set tonight?" Gina asked while moving one of her hands through his hair, the other, along the inseam of his jeans.

"Mmm," he responded with bedroom eyes, his thinking, a little fuzzy.

"Ricky," Jack's gruff voice woke him from his stupor. Gina stayed just where she was.

"Jack," Rick murmured.

"It's almost nine. You gonna set up?"

Rick came back to reality and jumped off his barstool. "Yup. Just got the guitar tonight, so it'll only take a minute." Rick grabbed a stool and brought it to the stage. After testing the sound and the mic, Rick called attention to The Tavern's regulars.

He'd promised them last time that he'd cover some popular numbers, so he started with a Matchbox Twenty song about needing someone, anyone, to cling to, when the chips were down. After finishing the first number, Rick followed with another MB20 song with a similar theme about one night stands. This one had him thinking about Gina and how one night couldn't hurt anything. It's not as if Lena exactly wanted him. He knew Gina was eager and Rick was definitely in need of a woman's tender touch. As he sang the lyrics, he saw Gina watching him. Rick realized it would mean much more than one night to her. She'd been attracted to him for a while now, and if he went home with her tonight, it would only cause her heartache. He finished the song and followed it with a sadder song about a girl with no self-esteem, and a boy who needed her to see just how much she was worth. But this particular Matchbox Twenty song was more than Rick could handle. He broke down mid-way, apologized for such a short performance, and bolted out of the bar, leaving his guitar behind. His only thought...fighting for Lena. Making her see how very much they were meant to be together.

"Rick," he heard her call after him.

Closing his eyes to gather himself, Rick turned slowly. "Gina, it's not a good time."

"But, I thought..."

"I'm sorry." Rick continued toward his bike and straddled it. "I'm sorry I led you on before, but...it's just not a good time."

Gina stood there seductively. "Okay, Ricky, maybe next time."

Faking a smile, he said, "Take it easy, Gina," then he took off on his bike and headed for Haledon.

It'd been one month since Lena had left the hospital, and two since he'd walked out of her room at her request. He couldn't take it any longer; her love was worth the fight. Even though it was Lena, herself, that he was fighting.

He rang the Giordano's doorbell, knowing, from a vain attempt to call her, that she'd been staying with them.

"Rick," Jules greeted him with her usual smile.

Rick sighed, "I need to see her, Jules."

"I know, Rick, but she doesn't...oh, hell, let's just try."

"Oh, Jules, you're terrific. Thank you so much." Grateful, Rick beamed.

"Let me just check on her, make sure she's...decent."

Rick felt his face warm beneath his skin.

"I mean, she does lay in bed all day. Let me just see if her hair's combed and...well, you know."

His stomach burned; it was now or never. Rick had to convince Lena that they were meant to be together...forever.

"Well," Jules frowned, walking down the stairs, "she looks great, but she isn't too keen on seeing you...I don't understand, you're such a nice guy. What did you do?"

"I don't know, I really don't."

Lucky for Rick, Jules seemed to be on his side; she gave him one of those pity smiles that screamed *oh poor poor chap.*

Following Jules up the stairs, Rick braced himself for a less than warm welcome. Not understanding why she felt the way she did, he at least hoped she wouldn't throw anything at him when he walked through her door.

"Hey, you," he said with as much buoyancy as he could muster.

Her scowl evident, Rick noticed the frown never reached her eyes. Sadness did. "Hi."

"So, you're on bed rest?" Dammit, he could've started with something a little more intelligent.

A single nod, before she averted her eyes down, he knew what would follow; he'd be ignored. Needing to grab her attention, he shut the door hard behind him.

Lena's head snapped up, as he expected. "Why'd you do that? Leave it open."

Rick disregarded her request and moved toward her bed. Sitting on the edge, he patted her blanket-covered legs. "You feel skinny under there. You eating enough?"

"I don't get too hungry sitting in bed all day. Why are you here?" She sounded annoyed.

"Well, you need to eat, so..."

"Rick," she interrupted. "Why are you here? You need to leave. And open that door, I want my mother."

Rick closed his eyes and inhaled, exhaling only as he spoke. "Don't push me away, Lena. Don't tell me you don't want me, and don't deny this connection between us." His heart seemed to stop, as did his breathing, when Lena didn't respond.

Exhaling as he sighed, Rick's heart beat picked up, and he felt a fire raging beneath his chest. He wanted to scream. Shake the sense back into her. But that would only push her away even more. Taking a few breaths to retrieve some of that composure he used to have, he proceeded slowly. "Lena. I'm not asking you to jump right into anything," he lied, knowing damn well he wanted to spend the rest of his life with her. "I'm just asking for a chance. We were meant to be together, Lena. Even if you don't know it yet, how *will* you, unless you give me a chance?"

"No. I won't." If Lena's eyes hadn't betrayed her, he'd almost believe she really didn't want him just by her stone-cold response.

"Why? Can you tell me that, at least?"

She leaned back on her pillow and closed her eyes. "I don't like how I feel when I'm with you."

The actual stabbing of a knife through his heart could not have cut any deeper than her words had. She disliked her own feelings when she was with him? How could that be? "You don't like...what exactly *do* you feel when we're together, Lena? Because until recently, you seemed to enjoy my company," asked a rather incensed Rick.

Unquestionably irritated by Rick's inquiry, Lena sighed, ignoring his request for an answer.

Now vexed to the point of needing to punch his fist through a wall, Rick stood from the bed and paced the room to bring his sudden fury down to a simmering flame. "Lena, work with me here. What do you feel? What am I doing that is causing you to be so...," he balled his fists in frustration, "...so...irrational."

"Irrational?" A heated Lena shot back. "I am not irrational...you..." Lena's hands went to her stomach, in a protective embrace. "Just leave."

"Lena."

"Leave."

"But..."

"Now."

Punctured and broken, Rick walked, shoulders slumped and heart sunk, out of Lena's room. Out of her house. And out of her life.

On his ride home, he stopped at some dive on Route 23. As cliché as it sounded, he needed to drown his heartache with a drink. Maybe two. When he walked in, Rick saw Jackie from work sitting at the bar. He gave her a bittersweet smile when she noticed him. Rick had liked Jackie. They'd met one day at work when he'd needed information about a customer. As Customer Service Supervisor, Jackie had provided Rick with the customer's details. After some light-hearted bantering, Jackie had asked him if he'd like to go with her to happy hour that evening. Unattached and lonely, Rick had accepted. They'd hit it off right away, and things had gone well, until Rick realized Jackie wanted more than just a date every weekend. She'd wanted a relationship. Rick had not. Still hoping that his long-lost Angelina would show up to ride him off into the sunset, Rick could not commit to anyone else.

He would have never guessed that when Angelina did show up, she'd want nothing to do with him.

Putting the past behind him, he walked up to the bar and addressed Jackie. "Hey."

"Hey, Rick, how are ya?" Her smile expressed a loneliness that matched his own.

"Hi, Jackie. How are you?" Rick pointed to the stool next to hers.

"No, sit, it's all yours." Patting the stool, Jackie's smile reached her eyes.

"Gin and Tonic, please," Rick said to the bartender, before giving his attention to Jackie.

"I thought you were a Whisky Sour man?" she joked.

"Yeah, well, sometimes you gotta change the way you roll," Rick quipped.

"So, what brings you here tonight? You usually hang at The Tavern on Friday nights, don't you?"

"Needed another change." In a hurry to numb his stinging heart, Rick swallowed nearly half his Gin and Tonic in one gulp.

"You come here often?" Rick asked Jackie.

"Not too much. I'm friends with Luke." She pointed with her chin towards the bartender. "I like to hang around and talk with him."

"Aah, I see," Rick winked.

"No, nothing like that, just friends."

"Oh, well, that's cool."

"Need another?" Luke asked, noting Rick's empty glass.

"Yes, please," answered a now relaxed Rick.

"So." Jackie started. "You get together with that chick from P.R. yet?" Rick detected jealousy in Jackie's question.

"Nah." Rick attempted to keep his gloominess to himself. Jackie didn't need to know his real feelings.

"So the baby's not yours then?" Jackie asked.

"Nope." Rick downed his second glass; Luke immediately hit him with a third. Rick started feeling good.

"You're a friend of Jackie's?" Luke asked.

"Luke," Jackie chimed in, "this is Rick, the guy I dated last Summer."

"Oh, yeah, the one you only stopped talking about like a month ago?"

"Luke," Jackie snapped.

Barely paying attention, Rick found himself caught between momentary thoughts of Lena and the comfortable warmth radiating beneath his chest. His foggy thoughts were a nice diversion too.

Suddenly though, he was all too aware that Jackie was sitting closer to him. He felt her arm rub against his, before her hand landed on his thigh. The gentle touch sent a pleasant sensation to his groin. When he turned to look at her, he knew exactly what her eyes were asking.

"I've only got my bike tonight," Rick answered to her silent inquiry.

"We can take my car, go to my place." The tremble in Jackie's voice did not go unnoticed.

Rick inhaled, closed his eyes and focused on the hand on his leg. "Okay," he rasped.

Arm in arm, they left the building...while Rick left his thoughts of Lena in the empty glass sitting on the bar.

Chapter Thirty-Nine

Still irritated by Rick's visit tonight, Lena sulked, wishing he'd never showed up. He only ever brought bad memories anymore. Since she'd awaken from the coma, she'd remembered everything about her past life. At first, like her dreams, she thought her imagination had fabricated stories based on Nana's life, but the feelings were more personal...and familiar. Her dreams were not really dreams at all, but flashbacks, becoming more and more clear. She knew it now. With every fiber of her being, she now knew Rick had been right. They had lived before. But, unlike Rick's view of it, remembering her past life was not comforting. Just the opposite. It scared the hell out of her. Her nightmares became daydreams, while she had been in the hospital. No longer did she need to be sleeping to fall back into her past. Overwhelming and heartbreaking, her past life haunted her. And every time Rick showed up, he'd trigger more horrific memories of a life she did not want to remember.

Including the darn murder Angelina had witnessed; Richard had been gone to war for about half a year when it happened. Angelina had been walking home from school when she heard a crack whisper through the air. Unphased, she continued walking home. Upon turning the corner, Angelina caught sight of a man. He was holding a gun. Beneath him, lay a man...who looked to be dead. Scared for her life, Angelina turned back and ran the other way, as fast as her thirteen year-old legs would allow her...but the man followed her. Out of breath and too tired to run anymore, Angelina turned another corner and slid into a tight alleyway. Her heart was beating so hard that she thought the man would be able to hear her, but she saw the man run straight past her, not noticing the little alley. Angelina crouched down against the building and cried. She cried for such a long time that the sun must have already set, because it was nearly dark. When she finally found the courage to step out of the alley and go back home, she took a different route, just in case the man was still looking for her. As soon as Angelina felt safe behind her own kitchen door, Agnes began her rampage, yelling and screaming at Angelina for coming home so late. Explaining to her mother what had happened after school did not do anything to cool Agnes' temper. It had only made things worse. Trouncing on her daughter once again, Agnes now blamed Angelina for the anticipated harm that would come to the Mancini family, dwelling on her the danger they were now all in because of Angelina's irresponsibility.

Taking her mother at her word, Angelina packed a knapsack filled with some essentials, and left home in the middle of the night. Unfortunately for her, a charismatic, older man had been the passenger seated next to her on the bus headed out of town. A man, who upon further inspection, only held the appearance *of charisma. As Angelina later found out, the only thing striking about Timothy was his hand.*

A piercing pain in her abdomen prompted Lena from her preoccupation with the tortuous memory. She feared something was terribly wrong.

"Mom. Mom," Lena screamed, swinging her legs off the bed, struggling to stand. She felt a gush between her legs. When she touched herself, she found her hand covered with blood. "Mommy, please., hurry," Lena cried.

"What, hon...oh my goodness. Sit back down, I'll call 911."

"Hurry, Mom, my baby." Lena fell to the bed, sobbing, afraid she was losing her son.

Her hyper-anxiety getting in the way of treatment, the nurses sedated Lena as soon as she was brought into the ER. After a few ultrasounds, the doctor called for an emergency C-section, so they rolled her into the operating room.

When Lena woke up, her baby was sleeping in Jules' arms. "Mom," Lena whispered sleepily.

"Sweetie." Jules brought the baby to her and placed him in his mother's arms.

"Sam...I'm your mommy," Lena said, as she kissed him tenderly on the forehead. The love that blossomed in her heart the moment she looked into her little boy's eyes was so overpowering, Lena thought she'd lose it. Never in her wildest dreams could she have imagined her heart's capacity large enough to love as much as she loved her little Sammy. Lena's heart expanded with consuming emotion.

"You named him Sam?" Jules asked.

With an expansive smile, Lena nodded.

"After great-grandpa Sam?"

"Of course. The way Grandpa Sam admired and treated Mimi, I want my son to be just like him. Respectful, noble, courteous...you know, someone to make his wife proud."

"Wife?" Jules laughed. "He's not even a whole hour old."

"Mom," Lena cried...real tears.

"Oh, honey, I'm sorry. I wasn't making fun, I just...I'm sorry." Jules sat on the bed by her daughter. "What's the matter, sweetheart?"

"Sam's gonna be alone. No father to love him and teach him..." So sad for her little boy, Lena couldn't hold back her sorrow.

"Lena, Sam has all your brothers and Daddy. He will be overwhelmed with all the *macho love* he's gonna get."

'Macho love' coming out of her mother's mouth made Lena chuckle. "I guess you're right." She used the cuff of her sleeve to dry her eyes. "Thanks, Mom...Mom?"

"Yes?"

"Can I live with you and Daddy permanently?"

Jules didn't seem surprised. "Of course. You never need to go back into that apartment."

"Thanks." Sammy started to fuss and Lena got nervous. "Oh my gosh, Mom, what am I supposed to do?"

"Buzz the nurse. She can show you how to feed him. You still want to breastfeed, right?"

"Yes."

"Okay, buzz, buzz.," Jules instructed, while pointing at the bed remote.

****

Her twelve-week maternity allowance ending next Monday, Lena didn't think she'd be ready to leave three-month old Sammy to go back to work. Though excited to get back to the studio, her heart ached with the thought of leaving her baby boy for eight hours a day. A single mother needed to work though, Lena thought. At least she was fortunate to have her own mother caring for him during the day. Grateful, Lena realized that she couldn't have done this without her parents' physical and financial support.

Thinking about going back to work would have to wait. Lena wanted to enjoy the beautiful, late-April weather. A stroll through the neighborhood would be a much better alternative. Lena put Sammy into the old-fashioned brown carriage Jules saved from Christopher's babyhood and started down Belmont Avenue. She loved Haledon, her hometown all her life. Lena waved through the window to Mr. Reilly, the optician and then passed the Campus Sweet Shoppe. Visions of buying red Swedish fish popped into her mind. How she loved those sweet little fish that came packaged in a tiny brown bag. As she passed The Pork Store, The Haledon Spa and then Mr. C's Deli, she began missing her childhood. More than nostalgic, she became sad for it, fearing for her future. She had a child of her own now and that scared the heck out of her. Some fears, she knew, were prompted by Vince's abuse, but some of them, like involving herself in a real relationship with Rick, scared her for unknown reasons. Yes, his presence sparked nasty memories of a life she'd rather forget, but his absence effected a sad existence during *this* lifetime. But would it be fair to Sam to start a relationship with a man who was not his father? *Would it be fair to Sam to keep such a wonderful man* out *of his life,* was more like it.

Maybe she was wrong all this time. Maybe she had Rick all wrong. Maybe...if Rick could ever forgive her superfluous, illogical behavior, they actually could have a chance to be together. Finally.

Chapter Forty

One more night of lying to Jackie, and to himself, was going to drive Rick over the edge. He couldn't do it anymore. Poor Jackie, involved in a dishonest relationship with Rick. He didn't have the heart to tell her that his heart still beat for Lena. Hurting Jackie again killed him. Tonight, he had to tell her the truth...before it went any further. After his set at The Tavern, he would take her home and tell her. But until then, he'd at least make their last date a pleasant one.

Rick picked up Jackie for an early dinner at Portobello's and then made way for The Tavern before Rick's performance. It was busier than usual, folks lining up against the back walls. The Tavern was packed. Some 80s songs were on Rick's set list tonight. He played for nearly two hours. When the crowd cheered for an encore, Rick performed a sweet ballad about losing sight of the important things, like love. A song appropriate of where things stood with Lena.

While up on stage, Rick could have sworn he saw Lena against the back wall, but his mind must have been playing tricks on him. Scanning the room several times while singing, proved the female figure had to be just an illusion. Lena was nowhere in sight. Disappointment affected him deeply. Oh, how he longed to see Lena again.

"Ladies and gentlemen." Rick tried his best to sound upbeat. "Thanks for coming tonight. I'm done for the evening, but as you saw on the marquee outside, I'm playing again tomorrow night for a special Saturday evening performance, thanks to Jack, our great host and owner of The Tavern." Rick paused to allow for some applause. "So come on back tomorrow and have a good night." Rick said his goodbyes and jumped off his stool.

"Ricky," Jackie exclaimed, the irony posing a sarcastic sting to Rick's emotions. What was that song from long ago? *Love Stinks?* Rick was putting his equipment away when Jackie hopped up on stage. "You were awesome tonight," she sang, jumping at him and wrapping her arms around his neck.

Not quite ready to break her spirits, he wrapped his arms around her waist and gave her a quick kiss on the lips. "Thanks, Jackie, that's sweet of you to say."

She kissed him again, holding him in the embrace a while longer. Rick allowed the kiss...though the twinge in his heart reminded him he'd be shattering hers tonight.

Breaking their embrace so he could finish packing up, he realized, though the crowd was dispersing, there were still people lingering and watching. When he turned to grab his guitar case, he halted. He hadn't been hallucinating. Facing him, with a huge tear running down her cheek, was the one person who should never have seen him in the arms of another woman.

"Lee, Lena," he stammered, when trying to speak. "It's not what it looks like. She's not my..."

But Lena had not let him finish, she turned on her heel and ran out, leaving Rick standing with his heart in his throat. Here he was, afraid to break the heart of a girl he didn't love, while crushing the heart of the girl he did. Right there, he knew beyond a shadow of a doubt, Lena showed up tonight to make amends. And now...he blew it.

When he finally turned back to gather his stuff, Jackie'd been crying her own tears.

"Jackie," Rick breathed.

"No. Don't. I understand. Uh...I was going to tell you anyway."

"What?" Rick asked.

"Yeah, I've been trying to figure out how to tell you this, but now...it seems you probably won't really mind."

Bewildered and impatient, Rick wanted to run after Lena, but he shook his head and stayed put. "I...don't understand."

"Luke...and me. We thought...we wanted to give it a shot. Ya know, see if there was something between us and all...anyway, now you can go to that P.R. chick and well, I don't have to feel bad for breaking your heart."

Rick knew Jackie wasn't telling the truth, but whether she intended to save his dignity or her own, he wouldn't push it. "If that's what you want," he said.

"It is," Jackie answered, much too quickly for Rick to believe she'd meant it, but he couldn't do anything about that. She knew where Rick stood now regarding his emotions; he'd let her lead him to believe she wanted out. It was the best he could do under the circumstances.

****

Saturday morning, Rick rushed down to Haledon. The minute he woke, he'd brushed his teeth, put on a cap and took off in his Jeep.

When he'd pulled up to her house, she was there. Sitting on the wrap-around front porch, with her hair tied back in a ponytail and covered with a glittery baseball hat, Lena was feeding her baby. He noticed her fidget when he moved up the sidewalk. Overcome by frenzied emotions, Rick barely ascended the front steps, dropping to his knees at the top, he cried.

"I need you," he wept.

She sat there, baby in hand, crying herself. "No."

"Lena, please." Rick rose and sat on the railing across from her. "It wasn't what it looked like." Cringing at his own words, he knew Lena wouldn't buy it.

"You *weren't* kissing somebody? What was it Rick, mouth to mouth?"

Damn, she had become much too sassy. "Yes, I was kissing somebody, but...I'm not in love with her."

"You mustn't really love me like you'd said you did, not if you can be with someone else."

"Lena, you're not a guy. Guys can be with someone they don't love." Oh, he was batting a thousand with his comments this morning.

"Goodbye, Rick."

"Lena, please," he pleaded. After a few seconds of silence, Rick stood up and, staring into the eyes of her little boy, decided to change course. "What's his name?"

"Sam."

"He's cute."

"Thanks."

Rick kept his gaze on Sam, falling deeper in love with him by the second. "Can I hold him?"

"I need to burp him," Lena frowned.

"I can burp him."

She let out an audible sigh.

Rick looked her in the eyes. "Please, Lena? I need to hold him."

After another sigh, she stood to hand the baby over. "Okay."

Rick took Sam from Lena's arms and sat on the wicker chair next to her. A feeling of amazement and serenity washed over him. Holding Sam felt as natural as breathing. Inhaling Sam's soft powdery scent, Rick kissed his velvety forehead. "I love him already," Rick choked.

"You do?" a surprised Lena inquired.

"I do."

"Why?" she asked, furrowing her brow.

Turning to look at Lena square in the eyes, he poured out his heart. "Because I love you. I always have and I always will. Not even death could prevent my loving you, Lena. No matter what shape or form you may come back as, I will *always* love you. You may want to push me away, but you cannot hold me back. I will keep returning." He took a deep breath and continued the dialogue he'd gone over in his mind time and again, hoping for the chance to finally declare his feelings to her. "So you can do what you want, push all you'd like, but I can't give up. I will not give up. And this little boy," Rick pulled Sammy tighter to his chest, "he's part of you. How could I *not* love him?"

Moisture welled up in Lena's big brown eyes, but she blinked them away. "If you'd never give up, why were you with that girl last night?"

He swallowed the lump in his throat. "Because I was lonely."

"You should have tried harder."

"What?"

"You heard me."

"Tried harder?" Now he'd become incensed. "*You* kept pushing me away." At first, his voice raised, but quickly he softened it, so not to alarm Sam. "How much harder did you want me to try?"

"You said you'd keep returning, right?"

"And here I am. What more do you want?"

"You wouldn't be here if I hadn't caught you last night."

Close to losing it, he fisted his hands. "Ooh, you are incorrigible...for God's sake, Lena, I was on my knees a few moments ago. I don't know what it is you want me to do here."

She gave him one of her stone-cold expressions, before her lips parted. "I want you to leave."

"Uggh. Fine." He stood up and delicately handed over Sam. He reached in his pocket and pulled out a small gold box, which he had wrapped in a red satin ribbon. Placing it on the wicker table next to Lena, he said, "This is for Sam. A keepsake." Then he turned and went toward his car.

Rick knew he'd regret leaving and he knew it contradicted what he'd just declared to Lena, but God help him, he could not lose it in front of the baby. He wanted that little boy to love him like a father, and he'd be damned if he were going to yell in front of him. Maybe tomorrow she'd be calmer...and hopefully, more level-headed.

****

Shoot. She should have stopped herself before getting so carried away. Watching him hold her little boy, tugged at her heart so hard, she wanted to grab Rick and never let him go. Why she reacted the way she did, she couldn't say. Well, she could, but it wouldn't be a valid excuse. Jealousy. Plain and simple. It reared its ugly head and made her gruesome. Seeing Rick kissing that girl, tore at her insides, tearing piece by piece, the very thing that held her heart together. Rick's love. Not that she'd known that before, but when Lena stood gaping at another woman in a passionate embrace with Rick, she had crumbled. His love is what had kept her going all this time; a sub-conscious effort she hadn't been aware of. A love that journeyed a century, carrying her through an abusive life, is what kept her afloat. Somehow, deeply rooted inside the very depths of her soul, Lena knew Rick existed. Loving her. Waiting for her.

Then... that kiss. When she'd witnessed it, she thought she'd lost him forever. Even though he'd all but thrown himself at her feet, Lena couldn't wipe the image of him kissing another woman from her mind. It drove her crazy.

In the not-so-long-ago past, Lena could suppress her emotions, allowing no one to know her true feelings. Now she found it impossible to hide them. Walking away from Vince seemed to change something in her, and she's not convinced it was for the better. Poor Rick, receiving the brunt of her wrath. She could not wrap her head around why she'd built this wall around herself. It was natural, she knew, to be wary of entering a new relationship after leaving an abusive one, but she did not want to be apprehensive with Rick. He'd never hurt her. She knew it with every fiber of her being.

Since Sammy's birth, her visions had stopped. If she were to be honest, after recalling her entire past life, the nightmares had slowly faded, until there was nothing left to remember. Lena surmised that her subconscious had been trying to divulge her story slowly, in order to heal. Once her past had entered her conscious mind, healing had been inevitable. No longer that poor little Angelina Mancini, beaten by her mother, Angelina Giordano had kind and respectful parents who encouraged her individuality. And no longer the Angelina who'd endured a loveless and abusive marriage, new millennia Angelina was able to walk away from her abuser and embrace what real love could be. These were different times and Lena, a different person. Her soul may have been shared with her predecessor, but she had evolved. Lena Giordano had grown from her past experiences.

So why wouldn't she allow Rick access to her heart? Why couldn't she just hand over the key, so he could unlock the love she'd held prisoner inside of it. She kissed the little baby in her arms, "Sammy, what am I going to do?"

With Sammy dozing in her arms, Lena picked up the ribbon-adorned box that Rick left for Sam. Curious, Lena slowly unraveled the bow and set the ribbon aside. She lifted the gold lid off the box, revealing a square of pressed white cotton. Placing the lid next to the red ribbon on the table, Lena turned up the corner of the cotton to uncover Rick's gift to Sam. Shaking as she lifted the keepsake out of the box, Lena could not believe her eyes. Every question she had. Every doubt in her mind. Melted away.

She held up the keepsake, examining the fragile gold. Her heart clenched as she held in her hand, material proof that Richard and Angelina did indeed exist.

The locket.

The faded image of the girl in her dreams stared back at her in yellowed black and white.

Lena's stomach fluttered. Her throat, constricted. With a trembling hand, she cupped the broken locket and carried Sam into the house. After placing him in his bassinet, Lena dropped to the couch and unclasped the chain that hung around her neck. Though the frail locket was old, the hinge still clicked in place next to its other half.

A perfect match.

The perfect symbol... of a love a century old.

Richard and Angelina, together again. This time, maybe they had a chance to see their love through. Lena wouldn't waste another moment contemplating this. Tonight, she would make things right.

Chapter Forty-One

Lena slipped into The Tavern trying to remain unseen, not sure yet if she wanted Rick to see her. Her body trembled with anticipation, excited to see Rick but afraid he'd reject her. After all, how many times will a man be asked to leave, before he's just not interested anymore? But fear would not hinder Lena any longer. She had a purpose for being here tonight. Lena needed to make things right and finally declare her love to Rick.

The three-foot stool up on stage held the most wonderful man she had ever known. Half-sitting on the stool, with one foot on the floor and one foot on the rung, Rick strummed the guitar laying across his lap. In the middle of a familiar song, Rick's deep velvet voice reached beyond her ears and to her soul. Closing her eyes, Lena let the sound enter her veins and spread like warm honey throughout her body. Never did she want someone so much. The easy grin on his face in between verses was sexy and inviting, and she didn't know how she could have even turned him away in the first place. As his fingers titillated the strings and coaxed the chords into fluid music, Lena felt the walls of her heart melt with every note.

His song ended and Rick, ready to begin his next riff, caught Lena standing at the back of the bar. A smile ear to ear spread across his face, leaving Lena with a mix of gratitude and a ripple of ripe anticipation. Immediately, Rick stopped playing and gazed at the woman who stood behind the crowd. All eyes turned to see what could cause Rick Murphy to halt his performance. Tempted to leave, Lena stood strong, holding her gaze upon his. She swallowed the lump that sat in her throat and managed a tight smile.

Not taking his eyes off Lena, Rick reached for his microphone. "Ladies and Gentleman, I'd like to play you a song I wrote." Rick hesitated, clearly anxious himself. "I've never sang this in public before." He seemed to swallow a lump that caught in his own throat, while his gaze never left Lena. "I wrote this for the only woman I've ever loved. I hope you like it."

After blending a few melodic chords on his guitar, Rick began to sing.

I've traveled far, I've traveled long
To find just where I might belong
I've searched the sky
I've searched the ground,

Feeling lost, never to be found
Then right where I saw you, standing alone
I saw my life, I saw my home.
In your brown eyes, I saw my heart
In my heart, I held your soul
Sometimes you find what you're looking for,
If you're lucky enough,
She'll be at your front door.
Sometimes she may be harder to find,
But in the end,
It was worth my time.
I'm asking now and I'm asking forever
To trust my heart,
'Cause we belong together.
So take that leap, babe, be with me,
Trust in my love,
See how great we can be.
Sometimes you find what you're looking for,
If you're lucky enough,
She'll be at your front door.
Sometimes she may be harder to find,
But in the end,
It was worth my time.
I'm asking now and I'm asking forever
To trust my heart,
'Cause we belong....together.

Her heart pounded, her breath wavered.
Rick wrote that song for her; Lena knew it. How on
Earth, could she have doubted his love?

Rick finished the song but left his fingers to parade the guitar. Slowly, his rhythmic short turned into a conflux of notes that sounded like a familiar song. A song about being in love forever and always, but what was he doing? She grabbed hold of her no longer broken locket and brought it to her lips. Rick continued to sing the lyrics when he stood from his stool. Walking through the crowd, inching closer to the back of the room, Rick's voice grew larger. He began the next verse of the song, flowing forth words about making vows and wearing white as he reached Lena. While lifting a hand off his guitar, he sang a cappella. Rick held out his hand for Lena to take. As he recited more of the lyrics, he led her to a nearby table. Sitting her down, still reciting the song, Rick's foot deliberately kicked out a chair, so he could sit. "Marry me," he sang. "Please." He stopped singing, set the guitar and microphone down, and took Lena's hands. Dropping down to one knee, he looked up into her eyes. "Lena, let's cut all the crap. Marry me. Right now, say yes."

Blocked by another knot in her throat, Lena couldn't speak.

"Please, Lena. I know you love me. I love you, I love Sam. We can be a family. Please, say yes." His eyes watered while they pleaded for her assent. He took hold of the locket in her hand and kissed it himself. "Proof, Lena. You wanted proof."

The crowd stood silent, awaiting, along with Rick, Lena's response.

Taking a deep breath, she found the courage to open her mouth, though she wasn't sure her voice could be heard. "Rick," she whispered. "Yes…I'll marry you."

Rick beamed.

The crowd cheered.

Lena leaned in closer, so only Rick could hear her, "But can we go on a few more dates first? Like where I'm not throwing up or anything?" She giggled.

Laughing, Rick picked her up and spun her around. "Whatever you want, babe. Whatever you want."

Then, putting her back down on the floor, he wrapped his arms around her waist and kissed Lena with all the passion that a man who had waited a century to do so, could possibly do.

Epilogue

Five Years Later

"Emmie! There's a pigeon! Right there." Lena enthusiastically pointed out the bird to her three-year old. Watching her daughter run through the sand chasing the pigeons couldn't be more satisfying. She'd named her Emmie, after Nana's MS-stricken youngest daughter, Lena's great-great aunt, who essentially was her own daughter during her life as Angelina Mancini.

On April 30, 2014, exactly nine months after Lena and Rick got married, Emmie Kate Murphy was born. The first time Lena held her newborn baby girl in her arms, she knew exactly what her name would be, and it was that much more gratifying to see her daughter running around effortlessly. Lena knew, deep in her soul, that Emmie, just like herself, now had a turn at a second chance at life.

Lena was burying her feet in the sand, while Emmie made the beach at Seaside Heights her own little playground. In front of her, Rick and Sam were playing Frisbee on the cool spring beach. Life couldn't be better for Angelina Maria Giordano Murphy. She had a wonderfully loving husband, two beautiful, healthy children, a summer home in Seaside Heights, New Jersey, and she was now helping students make music videos at Tagg Holland's music camp. Her cousin Mara had introduced her to her famous rock star boyfriend Tagg Holland, and he invited Lena to join his team at Camp Holland. She had finally found fulfillment in her life and peace in her heart. And Rick loved to point out that he had been right – the two of them were *meant* to be together. Not that her heart ever doubted it. It just took her mind a while to play catch-up. Her relationship with Vince had really thrown her for a loop, but he was safe in a mental institution for now. And Lena felt strong enough to face him if she ever had to. She'd cross that bridge when she got to it.

Presently, Lena could not be happier. She'd come to terms with her connection to her Nana and realized that their lives had paralleled one another's, but Lena was given the chance to make a change and take a different path than her great-great-grandmother. And though Rick's introduction into her life was the catalyst to her new journey, it was Lena, essentially, who had paved her new road and developed into a strong, self-assured woman.

"Hey, honey, why don't you come play with us?" Rick called from the ocean's edge.

"Okay," she answered. "Emmie, baby, let's go play with Daddy and Sammy."

"Nammie. Yay," little Emmie yelled, as she ran to her big brother.

As Lena enjoyed the playfulness of her enchanted family frolicking in the seaside's spring air, she couldn't help but be comforted by her own thoughts and her own certainty about life. Like her favorite carousel, eternally revolving to the music of the human spirit, life would never truly end. We would always exist. Whether souls were indeed recycled, or our loved ones carried on inside the souls of each one of us... life was eternal. If we were one of the unfortunate souls who'd experienced unbearable pain here on Earth, maybe there was the chance that God would send us down again, in the hope that we could learn from that pain– and learning, like the life of a soul, was never-ending.

The End

Acknowledgments

Thank you so much to my beautiful step-daughter Melissa Rappaport for your wonderful editing. Your keen perception and fabulous insight helped to tell a better story.

A big thank you to my baby brother Carmen Pellegrino for your help in catching all the mistakes I missed. I appreciate you taking the time to read my manuscript.

Thank you also to author Stefan Ellery for your wonderful help in editing and proofreading my manuscript. I can't thank you enough.

Thank you to my writing buddies, authors Kathleen Ball, Amber Dane, Jessica Musso and Stefan Ellery. I'm so glad we are going through this writing business together. You help me stay sane and on track. Your friendship is invaluable.

My love, gratitude and appreciation to my biggest fan, my mother Leanne. Thank you so much for your love, your nurturing and being the first to ever read my stories. You are the best cheerleader ever! I love you.

To my dad Jules, thank you for being my biggest inspiration. Thank you for teaching me, through your own example, to follow through on my goals and dreams...and to never give up. I love you.

And the biggest thank you of all goes to my husband, Johnny and my children, Matt, Sarah, Mary-Elizabeth and Christina. Thank you for your love, your support, and your beautiful smiles. I appreciate you all putting up with the many hours I spend writing and editing. I couldn't follow my dreams without your undying support. I love you!

About the Author

J.P. Grider (1966 -) born in Paterson, New Jersey as Julianne Pellegrino was raised in Haledon, New Jersey, the oldest of six siblings. Her love of writing started early in her childhood when she started writing poetry in-between homework assignments. As part of a school work-program as a Journalism major in High School, Grider worked as a freelance reporter for a local newspaper, writing feature stories about exceptional high-school classmates. She studied Television Production and Film Writing at Seton Hall University in South Orange, New Jersey where she graduated with a Bachelor's degree in Communications.

Two of J.P. Grider's novels have won awards in the Textnovel Writing Contest, with her recently published, Unplugged (A Portrait of a Rock Star) reaching Semifinalist position. Maybe This Life is J.P.'s second novel to be published.

Made in the USA
Lexington, KY
25 July 2013